SUMMERLAND AFFAIR

When geology student Alison meets Guy Kington, she is warned to keep well away from him. However, when she is stranded overnight on a remote island with Guy, she finds he is dangerously exciting. Alison realizes that unsafe coastal conditions are a threat to the foundations of the hotel owned by Guy's strange family. She investigates further and writes her own report. When a terrible disaster suggests Alison had been wrong, she is devastated.

JUNE SUTTON

SUMMERLAND AFFAIR

Complete and Unabridged

LINFORD
Leicester

L-2

First published in Great Britain in 1992 by
Robert Hale Limited
London

First Linford Edition
published January 1994
by arrangement with
Robert Hale Limited
London

The right of June Sutton to be identified as
the author of this work has been asserted by
her in accordance with the
Copyright, Designs and Patents Act, 1988

British Library CIP Data

Sutton, June
    Summerland affair.—Large print ed.—
Linford romance library
    I. Title II. Series
823.914 [F]

ISBN 0–7089–7510–0

Published by
F. A. Thorpe (Publishing) Ltd.
Anstey, Leicestershire

Set by Words & Graphics Ltd.
Anstey, Leicestershire
Printed and bound in Great Britain by
T. J. Press (Padstow) Ltd., Padstow, Cornwall

This book is printed on acid-free paper

1

RAIN hammered on Alison's sage-green anorak and bounced off her slim, now slightly stooping shoulders. She hoisted up the metal framework of her heavy back-pack.

She glanced up at the ominous, grey sky. "Summerland!" she muttered. "Humph!" But then an impish grin spread across her face. "OK, Summerland. Rain or no rain, I'm here and I'm here to stay whether . . . "

She stopped chatting to herself and held out her thumb as a car came her way. She knew it was risky — and Simon wouldn't like it a bit. A white Volvo sped past, splashing her jeans.

She was striding along the lane again, still not sure if she wasn't a little relieved the car hadn't stopped, when a maroon Range-Rover hurtled past. Then she realized it had stopped

1

some way ahead of her.

Her heart beat a little faster. She had not flagged him down, but he seemed to be waiting for her. A crack of thunder sent her hurrying towards the vehicle. She felt like an overloaded camel with all the stuff rattling on her back.

Later, she tried to remember what she'd felt when she first saw the man's face. The first lurching in her stomach. The surge like an electric current through her body making her nerve-endings tingle.

And it had nothing to do with the colour of his eyes. She couldn't make them out. Steely-blue? Indigo? It didn't matter. It was the expression under his heavy lids that collided with her senses.

She stared at him, the rain running down her face.

"D'you want a lift, then?" he said.

He tossed her rucksack into the back.

"Me next?" she laughed nervously.

2

As she untied the strings of her hood she saw him glance at her thick raven hair as it cascaded over her shoulders. She was about to unzip her anorak but thought better of it and slid her hand into her pocket instead.

His eyelids unfolded lazily. "Sure you don't want to change your mind?"

She wasn't sure.

He held out his hand. "I'm Guy Kington — from Cliff's Hotel in Summerland." His grip was tight.

"I thought this *was* Summerland. That's where I'm heading for. I'm Alison Lacie."

"Well, Miss Lacie, whatever it is you've got in your pocket . . . you can relax. I stopped to pick you up because I felt sorry for you. I wouldn't put my dog out in weather like this." He stroked the gear-lever out of neutral.

Alison reddened. "It's only my hanky." She blew her nose delicately.

One corner of his well-formed lips curved upwards, as if he was thinking a whole lot of things and not letting on what they were. In her estimation, those sort of people usually oozed self-esteem. She wondered how old he was. Thirty? Could be older with those spidery lines at the corners of his eyes. He was weather-beaten, as if he'd been around. Handsome though. She had to admit it.

Sitting straight-backed, he allowed the driving wheel to slide loosely through his long tanned fingers. The cord collar of his toffee-coloured waxed jacket was turned up. He probably thought it made him appear rakish. He was the type her friends at Polytechnic had as a pin-up. All that tousled black hair.

She looked away quickly as he glanced back at her.

"Hardly saw you in that jacket. Thought you were a tree."

Feeble attempt at humour, she told herself. Ever since she'd climbed in the Range-Rover she'd had a feeling he was having a laugh at her. Not a good old belly-laugh. He wasn't that type. His

4

type was all irony and clever-clogs remarks.

She stared gloomily at the bleak landscape.

"Cheer up. You'll feel better when the sun comes out."

"Does it?"

"Uh-huh." He nodded.

She supposed he was right. Unless he lived half his life abroad, where else would he get such a magnificent tan that made her feel she'd been shut up in a dungeon? Well, she had one day off a week in this new job and she vowed to spend some time on the beach sunbathing.

He interrupted her thoughts. "In fact, this part of the country is reputed to have a very low rainfall. Wonderful landscape, magnificent skies, wide open beaches — and where else would you find so much wildlife scuttering about?"

The words were no sooner out of his mouth than a huge bronze cock-pheasant ran across the lane in front of them. He cursed roundly and, clamping his hands on the wheel, managed to avoid it as it floated into the air and over a hedge at the last minute.

Afterwards when she heard him exhale, Alison threw back her head and laughed, her lips stretching away from her even white teeth. The gaiety spread to her rich brown eyes, wide apart and framed by a fine-boned oval face. It was his turn to study her.

"So where are you from?" he asked her.

"Near Newcastle."

"Wouldn't have guessed from the accent."

"It's not my home-town."

"And you're down here on holiday?"

He was sounding pleasant and interested now. And almost smiling properly. She noticed his features weren't at all even. There was a ruggedness about his square face and a strong jawline that defied anyone to disagree with him.

"I should be so lucky! No, I've got a job here."

"Where exactly?"

"The holiday camp in Summerland."

She didn't need to look at him to sense the change in him. She could almost feel him stiffen; see the bloodless knots in his knuckles.

"You know it?" she asked.

"I know it," he answered woodenly.

"I hope it's a good place to work. I'm going to be a waitress there."

"Oh, I've no doubt you'll find it suits you perfectly — except you don't strike me as being the type who runs to everyone's beck and call."

"Don't you like holiday camps?"

"Don't know anything about them." His lips made a tight line.

"I think they're great, especially for families. When I was little I was taken to a camp near Lowestoft and we had super fun."

He jerked to a stop outside some white gates with a gravel drive beyond. "So why didn't you apply for a job in

7

that area if you already knew it?" he asked drily.

"Because I like the one here, that's why."

He glanced towards a car coming out of the drive, its roof-rack loaded with cases. "They're making a quick get-away," he said and hauled out her rucksack.

"Have super fun," he drawled before driving away.

Children in the overloaded car waved to her and she waved back. Their week was over. It reminded her — she had arrived after the season had started.

She eyed a flag flapping wetly in the wind on a pole, squared her shoulders and headed for the reception area. It was to set the seal on her life.

Alison handed over her letter of acceptance to a woman wearing a striped blazer with a glittering S emblazoned on each lapel.

"Got your medical card, love?" she asked Alison.

A wiry man in his early fifties

exploded into the room. He was wearing a gold-flecked, open-necked shirt, with cream jacket and trousers.

The man's sharp, grey-green eyes focused on Alison. "Good afternoon, young lady."

"This is Alison, the new waitress, Archie."

"How d'ya do?" He popped a sweet in his mouth. "Haven't I seen you before somewhere?"

"I don't think so."

"I know! You was hitch-hiking in Coulson's Lane, wasn't you? Damn stupid, that. I didn't stop did I? Wouldn't let my little girl go picking up lifts with strange blokes, I'll tell you that." He crunched on his sweet.

Alison tilted her chin. What she did had nothing to do with him.

"This is a very respectable camp, Alison. I'd like to make that clear."

Before she could answer him he looked beyond her towards the open door and called. "Honey, this is the girl who's sharing with you. Can you

9

show her your chalet?"

A blonde girl enveloped in a shiny orange plastic raincoat nodded to Alison. As Alison followed her she heard the receptionist say, "I've got me fancy dress all fixed up for Friday night. I'm going as traffic lights, Archie."

"Well, I hope you won't be on red all night!"

The woman burst into giggles.

"Was that the proprietor?" Alison asked the blonde girl.

"Archie? Archie's the boss."

Through the windows of a building they passed, Alison saw tables laid for a meal. Cooking smells drifting towards them reminded her she was hungry.

"What time is the next meal?"

"Six o'clock. For the holiday crowd that is. We have ours after."

"My name is Alison. Alison Lacie."

After a long pause, the other girl responded with an almost inaudible, "Mine's Honey."

When they reached the chalet she said sulkily, "We aren't in with the other waitresses. Their block is full. I didn't know I was going to have to share."

"Which bed is yours, Honey?"

Honey pointed. Alison scooped up a load of clothes from the other bed, a man's vest among them, and handed them to Honey. "So this one must be mine, eh?"

Honey scowled, opened the wardrobe door and dropped everything in a heap in there. Then she walked out leaving Alison alone.

That night Alison went to bed early. She wondered why she was so tired. It wasn't as if she'd had to start work yet. Archie's wife, Rita, a timid little woman, had explained what she'd have to do the next morning, telling her not to worry if she forgot because someone would remind her.

She was woken from sleep by a loud whisper outside the door.

"I can't you fool! *She's* in there!"

"I'll see to her as well, then," a man's voice proclaimed loudly.

Honey spoke with a shrill laugh. "I can give you what you want!"

There was a long pause then the man said hoarsely, "Well, that's better. There's a good girl."

There was a shuffling, followed by a silence, punctuated by groans. This time it came from the back of the chalet. Alison stuck her head under the pillow and tried to sleep again.

Honey finally stumbled in and crashed on to her bed.

Thoughts tumbled in Alison's head. She told herself severely she was going to stick this job out whether she liked it or not. Heavens above, she was lucky to get it at all. But she remembered how Simon had wanted her to spend the summer at his house.

"Your mum's got enough on her plate without extra people around," she'd told him. It was true. Simon had brothers and sisters galore, all rushing in and out at odd hours. The last time he had taken her there she'd been utterly charmed by their happy togetherness.

She remembered too, the tiny thought that surfaced inside her. If you marry Simon you can be part of all this.

It was the sort of family she'd dreamed about.

Her father left them when she was seven. Later, she heard from kids at school that he'd run off with Dot Green who lived opposite their house on the council estate.

Her mum had grown more acid with the years. Alison never knew where she stood. Sometimes she was treated like a little princess, but at other times her mum would lay into her with a fist like a cricket ball. However much she cried, it was nothing like the sobbing that came from her mother's room.

Her mum was unlucky with men. When she did eventually fall for another one — a road engineer — he turned out to be married. Alison lay awake as Honey snored softly. Thinking was depressing in the middle of the night.

★ ★ ★

The next morning in the dining-room, Alison tried to appear bright and energetic as she copied the others and carried tea and coffee-pots to the tables. Twice she went through the wrong swing-doors into the kitchen and collided with people coming out.

She was trying to remember who wanted cornflakes, when the supervisor stopped her.

"Where's Honey? You share with her, don't you?"

Alison reddened. As she'd left the chalet, Honey had moaned, "Oh, my God, I feel terrible. If anybody asks, tell them I'm sick." Then she'd rolled over and gone back to sleep.

"She — she's not well," Alison stammered.

"Oh, I see." The supervisor saw Archie beckoning her from the other side of the dining-room and hurried across to him. Alison breathed a sigh of relief.

"Sick again is she?" a waiter murmured in her ear. "Mm — tell

14

her to give up the evening job!"

He glided away holding his tray in the air, his legs in their black trousers moving so rapidly he might have been on casters.

The room filled up quickly after that with everyone chattering and laughing and nodding to new acquaintances. As the clatter of cutlery and clamour of voices reached a crescendo, Alison twisted in and out between tables, giving a cheery, "Good-morning," to those she had to serve.

Some of the campers teased her when she muddled up orders, taking slimmers' breakfasts to those who wanted fried, and vice-versa, and forgetting who wanted more milk. Then, to her absolute horror, a heap of plates and their contents cascaded through her nervous fingers to the floor.

"Cheer up, cocky. You only die once," piped the gliding waiter. But it seemed to Alison that everyone, including Archie, was watching her.

When she returned to the chalet, Honey was not there. Her bedding had been left in a tangled pyramid. There were cigarette-butts in the washbasin and talcum powder all over the mat.

Alison sat limply on the edge of her own bed and remembered the neat room she'd left behind at Northside Polytechnic.

Simon's words came back to her. 'OK, Miss Independent, go and earn yourself some holiday money, but promise you'll let me know straight away if it doesn't work out. I can be there the same day to collect you'.

Dear, kind Simon. When she'd first arrived at Northside Poly, he'd taken her under his wing. Later, he'd said she'd looked like a waif. She grinned ruefully. She'd felt as lost then as she did now in this new job. But she hadn't been so clumsy!

Her large brown eyes clouded. Her troubles had been inside her then. Just before she'd left home for Poly, her mother had decided right out of the blue that she didn't want her to leave after all. Alison spent months writing long letters to cheer her up and listening to her tirades on the phone. If it hadn't been for Simon persuading her to carry on with the course, she'd have packed up and gone home.

If only she had!

She stood up quickly and wiped her cheeks, then she changed into pale blue jeans and white sweater. With a determined stride she marched outside past chalets and empty tennis courts and across fields to the beach.

"It'll bring roses to your cheeks down there. It's blowing a gale," joked a camper with cheerful familiarity. The man's wife added, "And the path is really soggy farther along. I'd use the path up there if I were you." She pointed towards the perimeter of the field.

Alison thanked them, smiled and walked towards the next field where the path was on higher ground. She stood on the clifftop with the wind teasing her long dark hair into unruly streamers.

Below her, the North Sea smashed steely-grey rollers on to the shore, sucking them back noisily, dragging in pebbles and debris and leaving shingle in steeper banks dotted with yeast-like froth.

With her pale cheeks whipped pink, she made her way down to the beach where some steps had been carved out. Was it heavy rain that had caused the edges of the path to crumble?

Without warning, her feet slid from under her and even though she was holding on to the rope-railing she slipped down. Some loose pieces of rocks rattled down to the beach. Shaken, she stood up and beat sand and mud from her jeans.

The beach was practically deserted, except for someone walking a dog. She recognized who it was and thought of turning back. No, you don't she told herself, you came out for a walk and that's what you'll do.

Guy Kington had looked large sitting at the wheel of the Range-Rover but she hadn't realized he was this tall. He came striding towards her, wearing jeans and a black, leather jacket with the collar turned up.

"You didn't take long to make an escape. What's it like? 'Wakey-wakey' and 'Goodnight, campers'?"

"I don't know where you got your quaint ideas, but it isn't like that at all," she said coldly, patting the Alsation which gazed up at her wagging its tail.

"So you've settled in nicely?" There was wry amusement in his face.

"I . . . I take a long time to settle in new places — but if there's anything wrong around here, it's that path." She glanced over her shoulder and inclined her head.

"Oh?"

"It isn't safe."

"Well, it is not meant for sliding down, skipping down, or running down!"

"There ought to be warning notices."

"There are. They say Private. It happens to be for the use of hotel residents only."

She followed his gaze towards a large Victorian building farther along, on top of the cliff.

"That?"

"Yes. Cliff's Hotel. It belongs to my father."

His tone, and the obstinate line of his jaw began to irritate her. She tilted her head. "You mean to say you don't even bend your precious rules on a filthy day like this when rain has made the other path so soggy?"

"I think you'll find an alternative path over the far side of that field."

"Oh well! Then I'll make very sure that's the one I'll use next time!" She assumed a sweet smile. "I assume the beach doesn't belong to you?"

"Hi!"

They both looked up. A man with a slighter figure than Guy ran nimbly down the path towards them. The

Alsation bounded across to him and he ruffled its coat energetically.

He looked at Guy expectantly. "Introduce me then, big brother."

"This is my brother, Neil . . . Alison Lacie. She's a waitress at the camp. She didn't know about the path belonging to us. I was just telling her."

"Hell, Guy . . . we don't have to go to those extremes. We've not bothered about that for ages."

"So I gathered," responded Guy drily. "There's a distinct gap in the hedge between them and us."

"Well, you needn't worry that I shall be using the path again," interjected Alison. "I've slipped on it once already."

"You didn't say," Guy said quickly.

"You didn't ask."

"Did you hurt yourself?"

She fancied he was genuinely concerned, but his 'them and us' remarks still rankled. The man was a downright snob. She wondered what his position was at the hotel. Neil grinned at her. "Well, I give you permission to use our path whenever you want, Alison."

As she smiled at him she heard Guy murmur something about opening the floodgates. He called the dog and remarked to Alison, "If you did any damage to your clothes, the hotel will reimburse you."

Alison noted how Neil glanced sharply at his brother. Guy looked at him meaningfully and raised his well-formed eyebrows. "OK?"

"I was about to suggest it myself," said Neil tightly. "Oh, and if you can spare the time, father would like to see you." He turned round. "I'll look forward to seeing you again, Alison. Sorry I can't stay, but I've a hotel to run." He smiled at her before running back up the steps.

There was no mistaking the two were brothers . . . the same long legs and slim waists, but Neil's features were more even, without Guy's toughness. Neil's hair was a shorter style, too. But although he was the younger, he appeared to have the upper hand in running the hotel, although Guy seemed the more dominant.

Guy was watching Neil as he flew up the steps. "He doesn't look as if he has any bother with the path, and I haven't heard anyone else complaining. Hotel guests seem perfectly satisfied."

Alison noted the way he said 'hotel', making it sound very grand.

"You run the hotel, too?"

He scrutinized her through half-closed eyes as if somewhat amused by her remark, and said lazily, "You could say I was general dogsbody. I've been away from Summerland for some time. My father has been ill. I came home to see him. And now, like you, Miss Lacie, I'm finding my feet." His eyelids lifted to reveal piercing blue eyes. "Just like you," he continued softly.

In that instant, his eyes held hers. Then momentarily, his glance shifted to the gentle swell of her breasts under her sweater. For the second time since they had met, she felt her chest tighten, almost like a missed heartbeat. Such feelings over which she'd no power, made her uneasy — especially in this case — but she was not sure why.

He clicked his fingers and the dog charged to be with him. Turning away from her, Guy lifted his arm in a casual gesture of farewell and sauntered in the direction of the hotel.

Alison started walking briskly the other way.

Soon her feet crunched the shingle-bank and then on to wet sand where the tide was ebbing. Just as she had as a child, she started searching for stones and pebbles, promising herself she'd come again when she had more time. This was a treasure trove. She might find anything: semi-precious stones — even a fossilized sea-urchin many millions of years old. Wasn't it this very coastline that had prompted her to look for a job here in the first place?

Then there were the famous Summer-land cliffs. Not in the pages of some text-book but right here before her eyes.

She gazed into the distance beyond groynes with waves crashing round them, out to a small island she'd seen from the clifftop. An island with a lighthouse on it. Gulls screamed plaintively around her. It was a haunting, doleful sound.

She made her way to where the cliffs were no longer a sheer suicidal drop to the beach below. Soon, she was clambering over dunes seemingly held together with marram grass. There was no way she intended to return via the path meant for *Hotel* residents only!

When she got back to the chalet, she stepped inside and stared. It was perfectly tidy; no clutter at all. Honey had even made her bed and was sitting at the dressing-table in a tiny, lacy uplift bra and mini-bikini briefs with a leopard-skin pattern on them. She paused in the process of stretching the wet strands of her blonde hair into a huge roller. She turned to look at

Alison. She smiled.

"Thanks a lot."

Alison was puzzled. Did she imagine that beam of gratitude lighting up Honey's face?

Honey continued, "I was coming from the toilet block and saw the dining-room supervisor. I thought, Oh, my God, I'm in for it now, but all she did was ask me if I was feeling better. You told her I was in bed, then?"

Alison was about to say it was the last time she lied for Honey, but then she checked herself. What she said now could put paid to a happy relationship between them and she, probably more than Honey needed a friend.

"That's OK." Alison shrugged casually and returned the smile.

Honey spoke with the comb between her teeth. "Is this the first time you've worked in a place like this?"

"Yes."

"Bet you aren't on the dole all winter, like me. Bumming around till May. You're a student aren't you?

Need the bread?"

Alison nodded. "Vacation job. I'm at a polytechnic."

"What's it like there?"

"Pretty good. Emphasis on practical work as well . . . "

"Bit different from here, eh? What d'you think of Summerland so far? . . . Rubbish!" She laughed.

"Well . . . I made a complete fool of myself this morning."

"Don't worry. When I started I was always putting the rings between the plates upside down. Had to be a juggler to balance the damn things. You'll soon get the hang of it."

"I expect so. What's Archie like to work for?"

"OK. Doesn't pay much but it's better than being on Income Support. Mind, I don't know how he makes a tiny little camp like this pay year after year." She inclined her head to one side, screwed up her eyes and scrutinized Alison. "Have you ever thought of dyeing your hair? You've got a good figure and ever such sparkling eyes, haven't you? But that hair! Men like blondes you know." She turned away to look in her mirror again. "What you studying at polytechnic?"

"Geology."

"Yeah?"

"Probably sounds boring, but it's not."

"Got a boyfriend?"

"Yes. He was at poly, but he's got a job this year."

"Geology too?"

"Yes — and he knows a lot more about it than I do." Alison grinned on a nod.

"I bet he's got letters after his name. Will you get letters after your name?"

Alison hesitated before murmuring, "If I carry on with the course." Simon's voice came back to her as if he was standing right there beside her. "You've *got* to go on, Ali. You worked hard to get that grant. Don't chuck it all away. I know you were knocked out when your mum died but you must rid yourself of this guilt. Her illness had nothing to do with you leaving for poly. Finish the course and then, when we're married . . . " He'd taken it for granted they were a permanent couple. Everyone had taken it for granted.

She owed Simon so much. She doubted she'd have got through those awful months after the funeral without him. But now she was right away from him and from poly she was surprised to discover she was not very enthusiastic about returning to finish the course. Odd thoughts had been drifting through her mind. Like, was her mum right? Where did all this learning really get you? Hadn't it taken her away from her roots? From the people and places with which she was familiar?

When she did return home, people treated her in a different way — as if she were a stranger. And she felt as if she *was* slowly changing. That was all very well, she thought, but you weren't quite sure where you belonged any more.

The only certainty was that she hadn't been at home when her mum needed her most.

"It — it involves so much work, you see. I mean, this summer I'm supposed to be working on a thesis about the environment, the coastline and that sort of thing."

Honey rolled up another section of hair. "Rather have a bit of fun myself, personally."

"I enjoy walking on the beach. I always have done."

"Is that where you've just been? God, it must have been cold and empty down there this morning." She switched on the hairdryer.

Alison finished changing, ready to be in the dining-room half an hour before the guests.

"True. There weren't many people down there. I did meet a couple of men from the hotel."

Honey lowered the dryer and looked up with renewed interest. "What were they like?"

Alison shrugged. "Tall. I suppose you'd say they were good-looking. Brothers."

Honey's jaw dropped open. "The Kingtons? The older one . . . " She lifted her hands in a cupping movement to the sides of her shoulders. "Big shoulders, athletic, hair blacker than yours."

"Yes — yes, like that."

"That's it. The Kington brothers. Aw!"

"So?" Alison gave a short laugh.

"The older one — he looks sulky, but I wouldn't mind . . . " She shivered. "Ever since he came back a couple of weeks ago we've been nipping down to the beach in the hope of bumping into him. He sends prickles up your spine, doesn't he?"

"I think he's arrogant."

"I've heard he can be snooty, but I know somebody who works at the hotel and he says he's a real good bloke." She added after a pause, "Which is surprising when you think about it."

31

"What do you mean?"

"Well, after what he did."

"What?"

Honey shrugged, as if suddenly thinking better of it. "Could be rumours of course. They've been circulating ever since he got here. But what I say is, Archie's done all right by me — gives me a job here every summer. So what's his business is his business. See?"

Alison didn't see, but she nodded. If she and Honey were to share this chalet all summer, she was going to keep the peace. She liked the friendly way Honey was treating her now. Even if it was because she'd lied for her.

"Well, I've bumped into him twice now and . . . "

"Where've you met him before?"

"He gave me a lift yesterday," said Alison, still wondering what Guy Kington had to do with Archie.

Honey studied her closely. She was about Alison's age, twenty-three, but her next remark made her sound years older.

"Look, I know I made out I wouldn't mind having a bit of a fling with him. What woman wouldn't? You've only got to look at the bloke to know that. But I reckon my life and yours are poles apart. After what I've been through, I can look after myself.

"But from what I've heard," Honey went on, "well, put it this way. Don't ever tangle with him, Alison. Don't *ever*. He's big trouble!"

2

HONEY gazed earnestly at Alison from under raised eyebrows. "Know what I mean?"

"He's not my type, Honey, so don't give it a thought."

Janet, another waitress, popped her head round the door. "You the girl who dropped the plates this morning?"

Alison nodded.

"Archie wants you."

Honey switched off the dryer and adjusted her ample breasts back into their half-cups. "Go on Alison, get going. When Archie says 'Jump' we jump — if we want to keep our jobs."

Alison was irritated to find herself running after Janet along paths and lawns to Archie's house on the edge of camp.

The house was made from Norfolk

red bricks and L-shaped with picture windows. Janet rang the bell and chimes played 'Oranges and Lemons'.

A thin barefoot girl in skin-tight jeans and denim jacket opened the door. Her auburn hair was piled into a top-knot and tied with a wide pink organdie ribbon; corkscrew curls dangled against her ears. Her sultry green eyes questioned their presence as if she wanted to know why they were there but couldn't be bothered to ask.

Janet tipped her head towards Alison and said to the girl, "Archie wants to see her."

"Dad's in the garden. Go round the side and you'll find him."

The door was shut abruptly.

Janet mimicked, " 'Go round the side and you'll find him'. Miserable kid. She could easily have told him we were here."

"Don't worry — I'll find him," Alison said.

Archie was bending over one of the

immaculate flower-beds. He pulled out a small weed, stood up and shouted, "If he can't look after this garden properly I'll get somebody else!"

His wife Rita, a tiny woman about ten years younger than him materialized from a nearby shrubbery. "He does very well dear. You know how quickly weeds . . . " She stopped when she saw Alison. "Oh — did you . . . ?"

Archie swung round. Alison was standing with her shoulders squared thinking there was no way he was going to bellow at *her*.

"Oh. It's you," he said then looked towards Rita. "This is the girl who dropped the plates. Didn't you show her how to hold them properly?"

"Yes she did," blurted Alison. "I just happen to be clumsy."

"You can say that again." Archie scowled at her.

"I'm sorry," said Alison in a voice that indicated she wasn't going down on her knees. "And I'm prepared to pay for the breakages."

"I'm not bothered about the money! It's not the money bothering me. It's your face!"

Alison's eyes widened. She knew she wasn't pretty but this was a bit much! Even Rita seemed taken aback. She was hovering near him fluttering her small hands as if she was hoping to catch hold of his words before they reached Alison.

"What's wrong with it?" Alison spoke with quiet icy politeness.

"It's your expression girlie. If you have another accident don't look so bloody terrified. This is a fun place. People come here to enjoy themselves. They don't want to see long faces, especially first thing in the morning." He poked his face closer to her and emphasized his words. "Everybody *smiles* here! I bet they all thought you was going to get the sack the way you looked. That's not good for morale see?"

"I'll remember next time."

"There'd better not be a next time!

Plates is money!"

"Dad!" The girl who had opened the door was leaning out of a bedroom window. Archie beamed. "Yes, Tracy?"

"I'm off to see Mary now."

"You said after dinner."

"I've changed my mind."

"Well you can unchange it pet. You're to have a proper dinner with us before you go."

"Dad!"

"No argument."

The window slammed and Tracy's petulant face disappeared. Red now, Archie turned to his wife. "She's always going out — and look at her — thin as a flag-pole. She doesn't eat enough. You never saw our Debbie . . . " He stopped quite suddenly as if it hurt him to carry on.

Rita placed her hand gently on his shoulder. "All young girls watch out for their figures." She glanced towards Alison with a hint of an appeal in her eyes. "I expect you were just the same at seventeen weren't you?" she said, looking at Alison's slim but nicely developed figure and nodding rapidly as if encouraging her to agree.

Alison gave a mumbled "Yes," but told herself all she could remember about being seventeen was a diet of work.

She'd wanted to stay on at school. Teachers had tried to persuade her mother to let her do so but her mum's boyfriend said he could get Alison a job in a civil engineer's office. Her mum insisted it was an opportunity that wouldn't come twice, saying, "If you do stay on to the sixth form, our Alison, there's still no knowing if you'll get a job at the end of it, then think of all that time wasted an' all."

It had been hard work with little time for either lads — or food-ads.

"Which one is Mary?" Archie said.

"One of her friends," Rita reported. "She told you she was seeing her today."

Archie grunted and then turned to Alison. "So no more breakages eh?"

"No sir."

"Call me Archie. Everybody calls me Archie. We're one big happy family here."

The window upstairs opened again. Tracy shouted, "Mary's mum has gone and got dinner ready for me Dad."

Archie shook his head. "Tsk!" Then he called, "Just this once then . . ." He put his hand over his eyes for a moment. "When is she supposed to be working on her A-level stuff?" He looked at Alison. "You're at college aren't you? How much work did you have to . . ."

To Alison's surprise, Rita broke in. "Young people have marvellous opportunities these days. I wish I'd had the chance to go to college."

Archie twined her arm in his. "You're all right as you are. You'll do for me. Being educated doesn't mean you can cook any better or look after your man any better." He patted her hand and looked at Alison, saying proudly, "There's no better wife than this one."

40

Rita gave Alison a secret wry grin, pressing her lips together and giving her chin a little jerk as if to say, 'Listen to him'. And if it hadn't been for the odd expression in her eyes, Alison would have put them down as the perfect married couple.

That afternoon Alison went for a walk along the coast road. A watery sun was doing its best to shine.

Her mind skittered round the subject of her thesis. She was as bad as Tracy. She was making all sorts of excuses to herself as to why she couldn't get on with it. She knew full well nothing would stop her if she was really keen.

She looked to where the tide was battling in. She'd read about the devastating floods in the area years before. So many people killed. So many buildings wiped out.

Her astute brown eyes scanned the coastline. Parts of the cliff were crumbling, especially where coast defences were inadequate. As she gazed at the arc of cliffs sweeping into the distance, words like chalk-seam, sand, gravels, jumped into her brain.

A man was walking his dog on the beach. A girl was running to catch up with him. She was dressed in denim jeans and jacket. Surely it was Tracy? And was it Guy with her? He put his arm around her.

Alison turned away and shrugged. Whoever it was, it was no business of hers, she thought. But before she started walking back to the road she found her gaze dragged sideways again to the couple. This time she realized the girl *was* Tracy but the man was Neil.

She was barely conscious of a new lightness in her mind.

Before long, she was passing Cliff's Hotel. Honey had said it was named after Clifford Kington, Guy's father.

Alison was not keen on rambling Victorian buildings. She preferred Georgian houses or something really modern, where sunshine could get in and lick the corners. I bet it's dark and gloomy in there, she thought.

The hotel had sharply pointed gables and steps that led up to a wooden-panelled door with stained-glass windows either side, and a veranda in front. There wasn't much she liked about the place, except perhaps the ornate red chimney, and that had a nasty crack.

She had to admit the hotel would have the most fabulous sea-views, positioned as it was on top of the cliffs. She had a bet with herself that one could even feel vibrations from the waves when there was a storm.

Then, for some odd reason, she experienced an uncanny sensation she could not explain — like the instinct of an animal when it senses danger. Frightening thoughts hovered in her mind. She gave herself a mental shake. She had to learn to keep a check on her too-vivid imagination.

As she walked on, she saw a stretch of grassland next to the hotel. She passed it and fancied she could hear a cry. She stood still, but could only hear the intermittent thump of waves on the shore and smell the tangy salt air.

But then she heard the cry again.

She hurried through the grass where hawthorn bushes straggled the cliff-edge. She gazed through them and down to the beach. Nothing unusual down there.

"Can somebody come?" shouted a voice. It was all too clear this time.

She ran towards the fence that doubtless surrounded the grounds at the back of the hotel and scrambled up it, scraping the toes of her trainers. As she balanced herself she saw an elderly man sitting at an awkward angle in a wheel-chair that had one of its wheels jammed between a rockery and the path. A red-checked rug had fallen to the ground and the man, who looked as if he'd been trying to pick it up, was hopelessly stuck.

"Hold on. I'm coming," she shouted and sprang down then ran back to the road and round to the hotel. Guests in the front vestibule stared at her as she flew past them into the hall.

"Man stuck out there!" she called as she hurried through one of the open doors to where she'd spotted a conservatory beyond, leading into the garden. She dodged between white basket chairs and tall potted palms to reach the man outside.

"Can you get me out of this confounded mess?" he snapped.

She tried to free the chair.

"I'm not totally helpless! I can walk if somebody gives me a hand you know," he said.

"Right. Lean on me then and I'll ease you out."

He stared at her slender figure. Her eyes were merry. "Don't worry. I'm stronger than I look." But the weight of him made her stagger.

"Let me do that," intoned a deep voice behind her and the next minute Guy Kington's strong arms were wrapped round his father.

"Spoilsport," muttered Clifford Kingston and a grin that was half-reproving, half-amused, spread across Guy's face as he almost carried his father towards the conservatory. He murmured, "Thank you, Alison."

Clifford glanced at him and then at Alison, "Yes — thank you, Alison." He looked up at his son and muttered again, "Home barely a fortnight and you know 'em all. Are you starting over where you left off?"

Alison wheeled the chair to the conservatory after releasing it from the rockery and Guy eased his father back into it and leaned forward his well-shaped hands on its arms. "Now Dad — what possessed you to wheel yourself out there on a changeable day like this eh?" he said gently.

Clifford twisted himself irritably in the chair. "If I want to go into *my* garden and look at *my* roses I'll go whether it's a storm or a heatwave."

Both men had the same lean features but age and illness had made Clifford's chiselled jaw-line sag and become less pronounced and his rangy shoulders were now stooping. His paleness made Guy's skin look even more swarthy at the side of him — and there was not the same luminosity in Clifford's blue eyes — but the fire of battle was still there and both men were obviously a law unto themselves.

Several guests hovered with curious concerned eyes beyond the spacious rectangular conservatory. From the centre of them stepped a tall willowy woman in jodphurs. She bent towards Clifford, her long fair hair falling to one side of her beautiful flawless face.

"Oh Mr Kington; are you all right?"

"I'm fine Kedrun; fine." He patted her hand. She turned her head from side to side with a worried expression. "We had no idea you were out there. It's dreadful no one heard you. I asked Guy to show me his wordprocessor and we were tucked in his room . . ."

"Stop worrying." Clifford tipped his head towards Alison, who was about to slip away. "That little elfin face popped itself over the fence when I shouted. She helped me." He slewed his gaze between the three of them. "This is Alison — she's a friend of Guy's."

Alison couldn't be absolutely sure there wasn't the slightest gleam of malevolence in the old man's eyes.

"I happened to be passing, that's all."

"Very fortunate." Alison saw Kedrun's eyes flicker towards her bright waitress's uniform and then towards Guy. "I'm sorry darling. I have to go now."

"I'll come with you," said Guy and turned to wheel his father.

"Where's Neil?" barked Clifford.

"Neil isn't here so you'll have to put up with me instead," said Guy with what Alison thought was a good-humoured manner — for him.

Clifford wrenched at the big wheels of his chair and began to propel himself, "And what good is that? I'll just be getting used to you when you'll leave me again. Won't you?"

As Alison followed Clifford she saw Guy talking to Kedrun, her face uptilted and close to his.

"Edna!" called Clifford to the receptionist. "Please give this young woman some tea." He nodded towards Alison.

"Oh no, I really can't stay . . . " she began.

"Too late — she's gone now," he said and indicated she should go into the drawing-room.

Alison found herself alone in there. If she'd thought the outside of the hotel was dreary she'd to think again about the inside. It was decorated with great taste and flair, with the Victorian atmosphere retained. There were deep rich colours — crimsons and golds — and the wallpaper was highly patterned with one wall covered in lovely miniature paintings and other small pictures with fancy gilt frames. At the windows were exquisite lace drapes. She bent to smell the perfect scent from a bowl of yellow roses on a small round table.

"So this is where you are?" Guy strode into the room. Now they were alone together, Alison noticed everything about him: the peat-coloured roll-neck sweater and that, like Kedrun, he wore jodphurs; his expensive gold wrist-watch and top quality riding-boots. Here was a man who didn't stint himself — who had probably never known a day's worry about money in his life.

"Like the roses?" He came to stand beside her and she caught the tang of his spicy aftershave.

"They're lovely. Marvellous arrangement," Alison said.

"Neil did it. He's the artistic one in the family."

She felt suddenly dwarfed by him, looked up and smiled shyly. "We — seem to have frightened your guests away.

"They are probably enjoying this bit of sunshine. Sit down, Alison."

She liked the sound of her name

on his lips. He held out his arms to take her anorak and she wished she'd changed out of her waitress's outfit before leaving the camp.

Guy lounged on a deep, floral, chintz armchair, stretching out his long, loose legs. She thought, this was where a man like him belonged — in sumptuous rooms, lolling idly and letting the world roll by.

"So, how's the waitressing going?" he asked.

She grinned. "You wouldn't believe it if I told you — heavens!" She stopped and gazed at the trolley being wheeled in by a waiter. It held a large, silver teapot and fine bone-china crockery together with enough food for about six people.

"I — I thought just a cup of tea . . . "

The chef will be tight-lipped all day if we don't demolish it. Come on."

As Guy leaned towards her holding a silver dish of hot toasted tea-cakes she took in the delicious aroma of home baking. She was hungrier than she'd realized and enjoyed the food. Between eating she told him about the incident with the plates. To her surprise he threw back his head and laughed.

"It's not your forte is it?"

"It's my holiday job — but I'm getting better at it."

"So what do you do the rest of the time?"

"I'm a geology student."

He couldn't have been more astonished if she'd shovelled all the cakes in her mouth at once. She admitted to a tiny thrill of satisfaction that she'd made him sit up and take notice.

"Good Lord!" There was no laughter now. His deep blue eyes were fixed on her. She'd noticed some people looked at you when they listened but not when they talked. Guy Kington was a man who looked all the time. Almost as if he could see right through a person. It could be . . . uncomfortable.

"How on earth did you take up

a subject like geology?" he added, curiosity wrinkling his wide brow.

She asked herself, how much is a man with his well-to-do background going to understand about someone with mine? I didn't follow in a family tradition of going straight from school to university as I expect he did.

She levelled her gaze at him. "From the time I was sixteen I worked in an engineer's office. Very boring! At first that is. I made coffee, ran errands — answered phones and then . . . "

"Then?" He'd put down his plate and nodded encouragingly.

"Well then they began to give me real jobs. I thought so anyway. Like printing plans from negatives and plotting bore-hole drawings." Alison paused and then added, "I loved going on site. Oh, I only did beginner's things, like holding the tape and that sort of thing, but when I'd been going to day-release classes I was able to do soil investigations and suchlike.

"Fortunately, I managed to get enough qualifications to go to the polytechnic." She stopped as she remembered her mum's reaction to that.

"Well, I could certainly have done with a grounding like yours."

Her eyes widened. She hadn't expected that reaction. Perhaps it had not been all private schools and college for him, after all.

"Oh, anyone can do what I did!" she enthused, spurred on now by his obvious interest. She went on to talk about her course more enthusiastically than she had for a long time.

"I probably inherited a natural leaning towards geology from my father. He was very interested in rock formations."

"Was he a scientist?"

"Well . . . no," she said aloud, but added to herself, but he might have been in another time, another place. She could remember trotting after him on holiday as he collected stones and pebbles from the beach. He'd told her all he knew about quartz and granite and limestone.

After her father left home, her mother threw out his shoe-boxes of stones. Even now, Alison recalled her own feelings of desolation. It was as if nothing remained of him after that. As if he'd died.

As Guy continued to ask questions, his sensuous mouth formed a smile, but she knew it was in friendship rather than amusement now. Was he being so nice because she'd helped his father? Or something else? Perhaps he just admired people who could do things?

She wondered again why Honey had warned her off him. But then Honey was inclined to exaggerate when it came to the subject of men.

Gradually the idea formed in her mind she'd like to invite him to the camp as her guest. Honey said staff often had visitors. It would be a way of returning his hospitality.

"I . . . I wonder . . . ?" He looked

at her enquiringly. She swallowed. "Have you ever actually been inside Summerland camp?"

As he frowned she went on quickly. "I'm sure you'd be pleasantly surprised — there's a lovely atmosphere — perhaps you'd like to come for a drink . . . ?"

His curt "No thanks!" came like a slap on the cheek. His deep voice sounded more aloof than she would have believed. She was furious with herself. After only a short time in his presence she'd been seduced into thinking he liked her after all.

He cleared his throat. "Alison there's something I think you should . . . "

"Mr Kington. There you are!" Two small silver-haired ladies hurried into the room. "We've just heard your father had an accident in his wheelchair. Is he all right?"

"Nothing to worry about, Mrs Bennet. His wheel jammed and he couldn't get out of the chair without assistance. Fortunately Miss Lacie here heard him shouting and came to help. He's fine now." He smiled at them.

"Oh that's good."

Guy had stood up and Mrs Bennet leaned towards him smiling archly. "Saw you out riding with your young lady — wish I was a hundred years younger!" She giggled as he gently squeezed her hand.

Her companion nudged her and mouthed, "Ask him."

"Er . . . Mr Kington . . . "

"Mrs Bennet?"

She ran her tongue over her lips. "Now I don't want you to answer this if you don't want to — but there's a rumour going round that you — that you're . . . " He bent low when she indicated she wanted to whisper to him. When he straightened up Alison noticed a slight frown on his face. He pressed his lips together and nodded.

"And you wrote all those bestsellers?" she gasped.

He placed his hands lightly on her forearms, saying softly, "I was hoping to keep it a secret. You understand?"

"Of course I do, my dear. You don't want the press pestering you on holiday."

"Dad needs peace and quiet . . . "

"And you can count on me." She held up her fingers then turned to her companion. "Come on, Miriam. And *you* can keep your mouth shut too." She turned at the door and looked at Guy. "But you will give me your autograph before you go home to Greece, won't you?"

"As many as you like."

While the two had been talking, Alison had been feeling a mixture of astonishment — and embarrassment as well. What was it she'd gabbled out? "Oh anyone can do what I did!" She groaned to herself. And he, a well-known writer, pretending he wished he'd had her grounding. Had he been laughing at her after all? Oh she wished she'd not put on such airs when she'd been talking about herself!

She swallowed. "Congratulations," she said with a sincere smile. "I had no idea you were a famous author."

"Thanks, but I was hoping no one in Summerland would recognize me. I've been away for a long time — even shaved off my beard." He stroked his chin. "And I do use a pseudonym."

"Which is?"

Her jaw dropped open when he told her. "*The Falkland Sound? Temple to Bacchus?* You wrote them?" she whispered. "*Monument to . . . ?*"

"Uh-huh." He sighed. "It doesn't matter how long one's away from a place, news leaks out; Dad and Neil won't appreciate it."

"I would have thought the publicity would be good for the hotel."

"No!" He barked out the word.

She was already stinging from his sharp refusal to her invitation and thought, I'm not staying around while he uses that tone. She snatched up her anorak.

"Alison . . ."

"I don't appear to be on your wavelength at all, do I?"

"Look, I'm sorry if I lost my cool."

"Perhaps if I knew as much about you as you've found out about me in the last few minutes I might understand!"

"I apologized!" he said stiffly.

"And *I* accepted!" At the door she turned unsmiling. "Oh, by the way, my dad worked on the railway from when he was fourteen. And we didn't have any scientists in our family and probably never will, unless of course I come up with something spectacular for my thesis — that's if I decide to finish this never-ending course for which I'm having to slog every inch of the way!" She stopped to catch her breath.

He was beside her in a moment, glaring at her. "What is all this? What's really the matter?"

"Nothing's the matter." She shook his hand from her arm.

He took a deep breath. "Alison, I was very grateful indeed you came to my dad's assistance but you must understand I cannot ever visit Summerland camp — if that's what's getting under your skin."

"I'm not in the least concerned whether you come or not!" It was the tail-end of his remark that incensed her and she added over-sweetly, "I only thought you might enjoy seeing how the rest of us live. Thank you for the tea Mr Kington." She stalked away from him.

★ ★ ★

Two days later the sun came out in full force. Alison spent any spare time sunbathing and swimming. Sometimes she and Honey played around in the pool with Maurice, the waiter, and Jack, who played the guitar and sang folk-songs and helped to organize the entertainment. He was stockily built and flirted with all the lady guests.

Maurice was bandy-legged and looked quite different from when he was gliding around the dining-room. But she liked him a lot.

It was after Jack dragged her with

him to help judge the Mr Knobbly-Knees contest and she finished up with tears of laughter running down her face, that she found the holiday magic of the camp was working its spell on her. It was a place where people could forget their worries.

She forgot about poly. She forgot about her thesis, until Simon's letters came to remind her. She told herself there just wasn't time to study — and to a certain extent it was true.

She always seemed to be rushing to get to the dining-room to serve the meals; to stand in queues. As the weather became hotter her feet began to ache and her clothes stuck to her body.

But there was always the smile; the big happy smile. Even when campers, cool in sun-tops and shorts, complained about the jelly and ice-cream that melted together into rivulets of white and crimson, she smiled understandingly and carried the dishes away to join more queues.

She started having horrific dreams. She'd been carrying too many plates full of sausages, eggs, bacon, kippers, ham, chips — runny jelly. And she always dropped them.

One night she woke perspiring. There was an airless musty smell in the chalet. She knew she wouldn't be able to go back to sleep and climbed softly out of bed.

It was bright moonlight outside and, wearing a sleeveless yellow dress, she strolled across the camp grounds. The only sound was of a baby crying in one of the chalets.

She crossed the field and was soon climbing over the dunes to the beach. The sea was like wrinkled silk, swishing hypnotically at her feet. She took off her shoes and paddled in the deliciously cool water in the direction of the hotel.

Suddenly she heard a muffled thump. She looked quickly towards the cliffs. A great lump from the cliff-face had fallen to the beach. She padded over the sand to look closer, almost tripping over the prow of an old boat protruding from the sand like a broken tooth.

Even as she inspected the cliff, more of it disintegrated and slid away like putty. She knew it was an area eroded by underground streams and high tides. Tidal surges could wreak havoc on this east coast.

All the time there was an uneasy feeling in the back of her mind. She tried in vain to remember the study sessions she'd had on landslips — on a similar set of circumstances to these. She shook her head impatiently. "Why don't I learn to listen properly!"

The worried frown stayed on her face as she made her way back to the camp. Then she saw a figure hurrying towards the hotel.

"Tracy?" she called.

The girl glanced round and pulled the small blue sun-hat over her face as if hoping that Alison would think she'd been mistaken. Alison shrugged. Tracy was no business of hers. But those cliffs were a different matter! She couldn't be certain until she'd spoken to Simon — and how she suddenly missed him — but she suspected something awful concerning the hotel. She ought to tell *someone* in Summerland. And she didn't intend to push herself at Guy Kington again! Perhaps she should speak to Archie?

It was a move she was to regret bitterly.

3

AFTER thinking hard Alison decided Archie was definitely the one to speak to. It was true the camp was in no danger, being well back from the beach, but he was sure to feel responsible for campers who used the coast road.

She never guessed it would be so hard to get hold of Archie. She'd no sooner seen him in one spot than he vanished again.

"Ha ha! Nobody catches Archie," laughed Maurice. "Unless of course he has it in mind to speak to *you*! Come on — talk to me instead!"

He grasped her wrist and led her to where people were running races. They sat on the grass licking ice-creams. Alison nodded towards his striped shorts. "They're natty."

My mother got them from her mail

order catalogue."

"Does she live near here?"

"Suffolk." His pink tongue curled round dribbles of ice-cream as they melted down the sides of his cone.

"Maurice — do you remember the awful floods on this coast? 1953 I think."

"Do you mind? I'm not that old!" He jerked his shoulder and pretended to be offended.

"Sorry."

"Huh!" he said on a grin. "Anyway, why do you want to know?"

"I was only thinking how vulnerable this coastline is."

"Sure. The sea has been known to break through the dunes."

"It doesn't help when folk wear paths across them — or drag boats."

"Well I don't drag my boat across there."

"Didn't know you had one Maurice."

"I keep it in Archie's hut near the beach. You can use it any time you like — but be warned — there are some nasty currents round here."

She smiled widely and thanked him. He crunched into his cone. "I — er — do happen to know a little bit about the 1953 floods. But only because I read about them! They devastated this coast; smashed concrete walls — and killed people. Mind you, we are partly protected by the cliffs."

"From what I can see Maurice, they're made up of material that can easily be worn away. Still, we're well back from the shore here so I suppose . . ."

Maurice rolled on his stomach.

My mother tells all sorts of tales — true ones too. Like the complete village that vanished in a terrible storm hundreds of years ago. Then much later, when the tide washed the sand away, you could see the outline of the whole village and . . . " his voice grew menacingly softer, "skeletons unearthed from their graves."

"Will you come in the two-legged race with me Alison?" Honey appeared wearing tight white shorts and equally tight T-shirt."

"Ooh, *I* will!" Maurice bounced upright.

Honey's mouth turned down at the corners.

"Oh blimey no. I don't want anybody with bandy legs."

"At least I wouldn't be running just to show off all I've got," pouted Maurice.

"Hah!"

Alison intervened when she saw Maurice scowling. "Maurice has just been telling me stories . . . "

"He tells everybody stories," groaned Honey "about the Roman soldier . . . "

"I was coming to the Roman soldier," interrupted Maurice tetchily. He looked at Alison. "There was once a Roman camp over the road where the pine-woods are now. There's a legend — whatever she says — that when there's an impending disaster, the soldier appears . . ."

"I've never seen one!" retorted

Honey. She giggled. "And it's not for want of looking."

"I can believe that," snorted Maurice. "And if you look behind you now, you'll see the current boyfriend. I expect he'll be only too keen to tie his ankle to yours. Come on Alison — I'll show you how to win a three-legged race."

* * *

Alison was jogging back towards the chalet afterwards when to her surprise Archie called to her from outside the snack-bar. "I'm glad to see you settling in now. How about a cold drink?"

She sat opposite him at one of the outside tables, sipped pineapple juice and eyed Archie warily. What did he want?

"You ever done any coaching Alison?" He unwrapped a sweet.

She shook her head.

"Our Tracy could do with some coaching if she's to get through A-levels and go on to college. I want her to have a better education than me — not as though I'm ashamed of what I am. Oh no." He moved his head slowly from side to side.

"Made my way from being a butcher's boy to owning a shop and then . . . " he looked around him and opened his arms wide, "I started all of this. And I'm not finished yet either. I've got plans that will put everybody round here out of business. I'm going to turn this into a massive holiday-centre — won't be called a camp then. And I'll succeed too. Know why? Because I can use this!" He tapped the side of his head. "And so could our Tracy if she'd only settle down."

"Of course I'll help her with her A-level work if she wants me to. I know how she feels about putting off studying. I'm supposed to be getting down to some myself."

"Oh?"

"I should be writing a thesis on the changing coastline."

"Well I don't see how you'll fit that in with waitressing!"

Or with three-legged racing, she thought drily. Aloud she said, "I will. I have to, because . . . "

Archie had turned away from her to wave to campers on their way to the beach with sun-beds and balls. "Mm?" he murmured.

She raised her voice slightly. "Because I believe the cliffs in this area are dangerous."

He swung round, his eyebrows raised. "What are you talking about? Dangerous? You'll start a flaming panic! Put folk off coming here for holidays! For God's sake! You ain't even qualified!"

She nodded. "I know. And I realize I could be wrong — but I still want to look into it . . . "

"You just keep your thoughts to yourself!"

"Surely it's better to be warned about these things? I was only reading the other day about a terrible storm

72

that caused a hundred metres of cliff to . . . "

"Reading!" He sprang to his feet. "We aren't likely to get conditions bad enough to wipe away great lumps of cliff."

"They're very soft. And I certainly don't think Cliff's hotel on the headland is particularly safe . . . " she began but he was talking at the same time exclaiming, "Before you start making damn-fool . . . " He stopped and narrowed his eyes. "What did you say?"

"The cliffs are soft."

"No — about the hotel."

"It might not be safe. The cliffs there are badly eroded. If there was a severe storm — a really bad one, the coast defences might not prove adequate. But as you say — I'm not qualified."

Archie sat down slowly. Another group of campers passed but this time he hardly looked at them. Alison continued. "Obviously I'd have to study them a lot more. My boyfriend Simon is very busy but he might come down."

"Boyfriend?"

"He's a geologist." She couldn't help adding, with a mischievous twinkle in her brown eyes, "A qualified one."

Archie ran the back of his hand across his mouth. "I dunno. Perhaps I haven't given this enough thought. I mean, if you think people's lives could be in danger that's a different thing altogether isn't it? And if you say you might be able to get this Simon down here to give an expert opinion, I'd be lacking in responsibility if I didn't go half-way to meet you."

She studied him closely. What was he up to? Why had he suddenly changed his tune? She didn't trust him one bit.

"What about your worry that visitors might be put off coming to this part of the coast?"

"I told you — I'm having second thoughts. I just realized, when this place is transformed into a magnificent complex with every top-class facility, people aren't going to be bothered about trekking down to the beach."

"Now, I'll tell you what I'm prepared to do to help you. You've already got one day off a week when you can get on with your studying; what if I let you off serving at some of the meals? That would help wouldn't it?"

"After all, everything that happens to this coast should concern us all, especially when it comes to looking after holiday makers. I'm giving you carte-blanche to get on with your study of the environment!" He leaned back chewing his sweet, his arms folded.

She thought, this is much too easy. But Archie isn't a person to make life easy. For anyone.

She pushed her hands deep in the large patch pockets of her pink cotton sun-dress. "Why are you really doing all this?"

His hands dropped to his thighs. "You've got a very suspicious nature!" He looked at her intently for a moment before pointing his finger and saying,

"*You* can do with my co-operation in this business — and *I* want to be the person you bring your findings to. See, I'd like to be the one who starts any campaign for better sea-walls and, er . . ."

"Stronger coastal defences?" Alison suggested.

"Yeah. Stronger coastal defences. And *I* know who to see on the district council. As a matter of fact, I wouldn't mind being a councillor myself, one day."

"And if *you* start the ball rolling, you'll get the publicity for yourself and the camp as well?" Alison tapped her fingers on the table as she spoke.

"Centre. That's what it will be, or complex. Not camp. Anyway, I'll decide when it's time to see the council, and in the meantime, we keep all this strictly between ourselves."

"But, when . . . ?"

He leaned across and put his hand over hers. "We don't want to start a panic, do we? Not till we're a hundred

per cent sure about this cliff business."
He tapped his head again. "We got to
use our noddles. You just bring me
all your findings. Oh, and get that
boyfriend of yours down here. I'm
not saying I haven't got confidence
in a woman, but I'd like to hear what
he's got to say . . . him being qualified
an' all."

What was wrong in him seeking
publicity? Alison asked herself, as long
as something was being done about the
situation.

"I — er, don't mind if you tell
the others I'm giving you time off
to study," Archie said nonchalantly.
"They all know I'm a great believer
in education. I'll just go and see Lorna
about it."

After he'd left, Alison cupped her
chin in her hands, as her thoughts
began to weave unfamiliar patterns.

With the extra time she'd have,
anything was possible. I could produce
a really valuable piece of work if I'm
right about the cliffs, she thought.

Valuable to everybody, not only me. It wouldn't just be your average sort of student's thesis. It would be special. Who knows, there might be reports about Archie and me in the local paper — even the national papers — for bringing this to everyone's attention. I'd really be on the way to becoming a geologist then. Perhaps even a famous one! The idea excited her.

She smiled to herself. She had never considered anything like it before. She gave her head a little tap and grinned to herself. She couldn't wait to get cracking.

★ ★ ★

In her ice-blue jeans and yellow T-shirt, Alison carefully picked her way along the cliff incline in front of the hotel. She knocked a small wooden peg into the thick sand and gravel surface. Then she moved farther along and did the same thing again.

When there was a row of pegs, she

bent down and made sure they were in a straight line. She stood up and scrambled towards a path that led to the top of the incline. She was brushing down her jeans when a deep, amused voice, asked, "Been exploring?"

She jerked herself upright and felt colour stream into her cheeks when she saw Guy leaning his long body languidly against a white gate at the end of the hotel grounds. She felt guilty.

"I — I was having a look at the cliffs."

"Find anything interesting?"

"T . . . too soon to say."

"Let me know if you do find anything dramatic. It's all grist to my mill."

"Of course — for your books. I'll tell you if I find anything really gruesome." She lowered the pitch of her voice. "Like the skeleton of someone who died in mysterious . . ."

She stopped. The expression on his handsome face had changed and now he was staring out to sea, his eyes bleak.

"Although I don't know if you write mysteries . . . " Her voice trailed off weakly.

He looked quickly in her direction. "Oh — yes — sometimes. But if I were you I'd be careful it's not your body anyone finds. Ridiculous to go scrambling round down there. Leaving the path."

"They aren't safe then? These cliffs?"

"Are you an experienced climber?"

"No."

"Then of course they aren't damn-well safe."

He opened the gate and went out to the pathway to stand beside her. Buttons on his cream linen shirt were undone as if he'd thrown it on after sun-bathing and she could see the sable-coloured hairs glistening on his expansive chest. His skin-tight jeans followed every contour of his body.

Alison had never been so close to a man with such a figure. She'd seen men like him on films and television of course. That was the best way. This way gave her a feeling of wanting to rush away from her own heartbeat.

His skin was richly tanned as if he'd been born brown. With his physique he could have stretched out his long arms, picked her up and tossed her to land on the shore.

She began to chatter self-consciously. "Did you know the sea level is rising?"

"Is your mind always on work?"

She blushed and fingered the rest of the pegs and string in her pocket.

He folded his arms. "I think we had a silly misunderstanding the last time we met. These things happen and . . ."

"Don't give it another thought," she said brightly. "You obviously had reasons for not wanting to visit Summerland camp. Let's leave it at that."

She turned to walk away.

"No, let's not. I'd like to talk to you about it. How about coming for supper on Friday? Or would that mean you'd miss end-of-week jollies?"

He had to get in a dig didn't he? she thought. "I would miss Friday night fun as a matter of fact. There's usually a fancy-dress party. Thank you all the same. Some other time perhaps?" She gave him a cool smile.

"Is it Alison?" said a voice she recognized as Clifford's. Neil was wheeling his father towards them. They'd come across the patch of ground beside the hotel where a wide path had been worn by holidaymakers when they took a short cut to the cliff top.

"Hello Mr Kington. Are you well?" Alison said.

"Enjoy your outing Dad?" said Guy.

Clifford's face was impassive. He looked at Alison. "Has my son invited you for supper on Friday?"

She thought, so it wasn't Guy's idea. She ignored a small stab of disappointment. Guy opened the gate saying, "She can't make it Dad."

"Surely you can make one evening?"

Clifford was frowning. He jerked at the big wheels of his chair to turn it towards her. Neil had been day-dreaming but now started visibly as the chair moved. Clifford repeated the offer and Neil added, "We'd like to repay you for coming to Dad's help."

"Oh but there's no need . . . " she began.

"It's nothing to do with repayment! Don't be tactless Neil," snapped Clifford. Alison felt acutely uncomfortable to see Neil flush but Guy quickly intervened and remarked quietly, "It's both gratitude and a desire for your company."

Pretty words she thought. Did he really mean them or was he simply coming to the rescue? Clifford gave a quick nod of agreement but Neil pushed the wheelchair towards the gate, then stared stonily at Guy and muttered, "You want to take it?"

"While you're both deciding what to do with me I still want to know from Alison when she's coming for supper?" Clifford announced. Alison saw where Guy got his brusque manner. She smiled evenly. "I could make a Saturday night — say a week on Saturday."

"We'll expect you." Clifford frowned and looked suddenly uncomfortable as Guy stepped forward to push him. "Neil can take me."

"Sure." Guy shrugged and stepped to one side. He gave the impression of being unconcerned but Alison noticed a moment when his clear blue eyes dulled. From an outsider's point of view it seemed Clifford Kington enjoyed lording it over his younger son but ignored his elder. Almost as if he was in awe of him — or was angry with him? She wasn't sure which.

As Neil pushed his father towards the conservatory at the back of the house Guy turned towards her. "On Saturdays we join our guests in a supper dance. You'll enjoy that."

"Yes," she said, wondering if she would.

"Will — will Kedrun be there?" she said casually.

It was an absolute shock to her system when he suddenly tilted her small chin with his finger.

"No, Kedrun won't be there," he said softly.

She realized she had given him *entirely* the wrong impression! He obviously thought she was attracted to him. Wanted him to herself even. She felt mortified!

Except for her well-shaped breasts, she had a slim, almost coltish figure, but now, under his long exploring gaze, her weight felt too much for her legs to carry.

The whole way back to the camp she tried, unsuccessfully, to rid herself of the feel of his touch on her skin.

★ ★ ★

"You're bloody well what?" bawled Honey.

"It's not such a big deal! I'm only

85

going for supper with them." Alison tossed aside the letter she'd been writing to Simon.

"Well, I wouldn't tell Archie what you're about!"

"What on earth has it got to do with Archie?"

"You'll find out!"

Honey leaned out of the chalet window and hung a pair of freshly washed briefs on the small plastic clothes drier attached to the frame. She dropped back on to her bed.

Alison had a job to stop herself yelling, too. Every time she mentioned Guy, Honey hinted at some mysterious happening she was not at liberty to talk about.

But now, she looked hard at Alison and exclaimed, "OK. I suppose I'd better tell you, being as you haven't taken a blind bit of notice of a single thing I've said. I only know what I've been told. You understand?" Honey tucked her bare feet under her. "There have been rumours flying for years, all to do with Archie's daughter."

"Tracy?"

"No. Debbie, his eldest. It seems Guy Kington was a bit of a lad when he was younger. That was before Archie started this place. He had a shop near here at the time it all happened. Debbie and Guy were crazy about each other. But Guy must have done something awful because . . . she was found dead."

"Oh, no!"

"Killed herself . . . they say. There were enquiries of course, because he was with her at the time! Terrible scandal. That's why he left Summerland. Joined the marines. I think he went to the Falklands.

"He didn't come back until his dad was taken bad. Archie never got over what happened. He hates them all — the Kingtons — especially that Guy."

"I can't believe it would be Guy's fault!"

"There you are. Hooked! That's how

it happened to Debbie — and you were so sure . . ."

"I'm certainly not hooked! That's a wild assumption."

"She was crazy about him, she didn't want to live any more after he spurned her." Honey's voice lowered as she whispered hoarsely, "He was her sole reason for living."

Alison frowned. "Are you quite sure about all this?"

"You don't have to believe it if you don't want! That's your privilege — just as it's your funeral if you carry on seeing Guy Kington."

"How do the Kingtons feel about Archie and his family?" asked Alison, wondering at the same time what Archie would say if he knew Tracy was seeing Neil.

"Well none of them speak to one another. After Debbie died Archie was shattered. Later on he sold the shop and started up the camp. I suppose it took trade away from the hotel. Perhaps that's what he wanted. Mind, it seems to be doing all right now doesn't it? Neil Kington's been running the place since his father's been . . . " She stopped and looked hard at Alison. "What's up?"

Alison had been staring at the ground, her teeth nipping her lower lip, thinking, had Archie been telling her a pack of lies after all? Had he latched on to her remarks about the cliffs because he wanted to see the hotel closed down? The Kingtons getting their just desserts?

If it was the case should it make any difference to her?

"N-nothing's wrong. I — I was only thinking about a conversation I had with Archie." She fingered the letter she'd been writing and said nonchalantly, "I didn't tell you did I that he's giving me some time off from work to do my thesis?"

She knew the minute she'd spoken she'd made a mistake. Honey cocked her head pertly to one side. "Well isn't that nice for you? That'll go down ever so well with the other girls!" she answered sarcastically.

Alison wanted to tell her why — and she almost did until she told herself it was the daftest thing she could do — to let it be known she thought the area was in for a major landslip. That would be downright irresponsible, especially before Simon had seen it. And even if he agreed with her, there was still a lot of work to be done in the way of detailed studies.

Honey began to dress. "So why has the old devil given you time off, eh? He's never done that before. Not to anybody. Especially not to me — and I've been working for him for years. Fat lot of good it's done me."

"But I've told you . . . "

"Archie's got a motto. He says it's one of his dad's. 'If the' does owt for nowt, do it for the 'self'." So, you tell me, what's in it for Archie?"

"He's interested in . . . "

"Geology?" Honey pulled a face. "No."

"Or should I say *who* is he interested in? I may as well tell you, it hasn't gone unnoticed that you and Archie were seen having a drink together at Willy's bar — and at one point Archie held your hand!"

"Janet says you were ages with him in his back garden, too. By God, you're a dark horse. You look as if butter wouldn't melt . . . " Honey snapped up her skirt zip.

Alison couldn't believe what she was hearing. She couldn't make up her mind whether to laugh or not.

"How about telling us what the secret is, then perhaps some of us old hands might get time off, too?"

"Honey!" exclaimed Alison.

Honey snapped, "Even *I* don't throw myself at married men — or those suspected of killing schoolgirls!"

Later that day Alison noticed Honey whispering with other waitresses in the dining-room and knew she was in for a bleak time.

One evening Archie stopped to speak

to her when she was vacuuming the floor after the meal.

"I told you you could have tonight off. What's happening about the project we spoke about? Why aren't you getting on with it?"

She switched off the cleaner and said awkwardly, "There's not a lot I can do at this stage."

"Well there won't be. Not while you're here!"

"I've got to go and look at the reference books in the library sometime," she mumbled.

"Well go then! Take the day off girlie."

Honey and Janet were passing and exchanged glances. Alison groaned inside.

After they'd gone she drew in her breath and said, "This is going to lead to a lot of ill-feeling Archie — me disappearing when I should be working in here."

"I run this place. I decide what happens here. Now put down that damn cleaner and let somebody else take over." He turned round and crooked his finger, calling, "Honey — come here. I've got a little job for you."

★ ★ ★

It was Saturday. Changeover day. Holidaymakers she'd got to know and like were going home. The van with clean linen was being driven around. Cleaners were changing beds and leaving chalets pine-fresh.

Alison felt curiously lonely. And then, to her astonishment, she saw Simon.

"It's only a flying-visit — a surprise," he said as she flung her arms round him. "I'm on my way to a conference . . . oh Ali . . . I miss you like hell."

In the security of his arms, his kind familiar face close to hers, she felt warm and safe and closed her eyes, allowing his kiss to linger. His lips were cool. And comforting.

She took him into her chalet and he

clasped her to him again, tighter this time. "Missed me?"

She nodded and stroked the back of his neck, her finger-tips touching his short sandy hair.

He murmured, "If you do that again I'll have you down on that silly little bed before . . . "

That was when Honey burst in.

Later the two of them walked together on the beach near the cliffs. Alison told him about the conversation she'd had with Archie. "I feel he's using me to wreak his revenge on the Kington family."

"What does it matter what his motives are? If a building is unsafe then it *should* be closed. There's no need for you to concern yourself in any sort of feud between these two families. Just keep personalities out of it. Do what you've got to do and keep the boss informed. He's the one you're working for after all. The one who's paying you."

All the time he'd been speaking he'd

been looking about him at the cliffs. "You've got the chance of a lifetime here Ali. You could turn in one hell of a thesis." He seemed to drift into a world of his own, muttering about glacial deposits.

"What d'you think Simon?"

"Any exposure of strata?"

"Yes — where they put in a pipe-line."

He stopped walking and stood looking at her. "Why are we wasting precious time? I've got to go soon. Come here!"

He pulled her with him into a crevice and kissed her again. The sun was on her back. In the distance she could hear sea-gulls crying.

She could almost imagine she and Simon were on holiday together. It was a lovely relaxing feeling.

"Hold me close Si," she whispered, wondering why she was being unusually clingy.

"Will I?" His lips came down again on hers. Harder this time.

She murmured, "You're always the

same aren't you? Always dependable."

"I wish I could stay longer . . ."

She glanced up at the cliff where they were standing. "There's subaerial denudation . . . "

"Eh?" He blinked.

"What?"

"Hell Ali — I was about to kiss you again!"

"I'm sorry. I've got these damn cliffs on the brain."

He sighed. "Come on then! Let's go and see if any of those pegs have moved."

* * *

It seemed to her in no time at all Simon had to leave. Archie insisted they had coffee with him and Rita first. He listened intently to everything Simon had to say, not understanding some technical terms but glued to his words, especially when the hotel was mentioned.

The next day he said to Alison,

96

"That was a clever young bloke, that Simon. Pity he couldn't stop to do a bit more investigating on the beach. But he doesn't like the look of things at all does he? I heard him tell you to keep in touch by phone. When is he coming again?"

"As soon as he can, but he's so tied up at the moment. He's just started a new job."

Rita was hovering near Archie and said, "I do hope we don't have any of those dreadful storms he was telling us about. I'll be keeping a close eye on my barometer from now on, especially when there're high winds and spring tides."

Archie gaped. "What do you know about it?"

"I was listening to what he said Arch. I never knew groynes in one part of the beach could sometimes make it worse in another . . . "

Archie ignored her. "If I'm going to take this matter of the cliffs further, Alison, I want confirmation of the situation from a qualified bloke, so you remind Simon of that when you write to him. In the meantime I suppose I'll have to wait for your findings."

"I suppose you will," she said drily. She turned to go.

Archie added as an afterthought, "And tell that Honey not to go hanging her knickers from the chalet window."

Suddenly Alison was fed up with him telling her what she could or could not do. "No. *You* tell her."

"She's your mate isn't she?" he snapped.

"I'm not exactly flavour of the month with the other girls. Not with skipping my duties."

"We all have to make sacrifices for the common good."

"Well I'm not taking any more time off Archie — and if it means I can't get as much done — it can't be helped." As she began to march away she caught a glimpse of Rita staring at her with her mouth open.

The next day when she had some

free time after leaving the dining-room Alison chose to ignore all thoughts of studying. It had even crossed her mind not to bother at all with the thesis. Never mind what Simon had said — personalities couldn't be ignored. Archie was too interfering — and she was already involved with the Kingtons.

She'd thought a lot about Guy Kington since Honey had told her about him and Debbie. She couldn't help it. What dreadful thing had happened to cause such a tragedy?

Wearing a pale-blue bikini she joined campers on the beach. She was splashing in the sea when she saw Neil. He was an enigma to her. Sometimes he seemed dreamy and withdrawn but other times he was full of life.

Now he was running and cavorting with the dog. He spotted her and shouted, "Hi Alison!"

The next minute he was racing into the water towards her in his plimsolls and shorts. She laughed and then squealed as he rushed at her. Swimming away from him she suddenly spotted Tracy watching them. Alison beckoned her to join them but Tracy stormed away.

That evening Alison stood alone on the edge of the cliffs gazing at the stars. She thought she saw a light in the disused lighthouse on the island but it vanished. I've been listening to too many of Maurice's stories — I'll be seeing a Roman soldier next! she told herself.

There was a sound behind her. She turned quickly. Her heart pounded as Guy's tall figure loomed. But his voice was ice-cold.

"And what the hell do you think you've been playing at?"

4

"WHAT on earth . . . ?" she began.

"Don't pretend you don't know what I'm talking about." He was glowering.

"Get out of my way please!" She stepped to one side but he still blocked her way.

"Sure — when you tell me what sort of underhand game you're playing here."

"Even if I knew what you're talking about — which I don't — I'm not prepared to explain . . . "

"I've known hundreds of women in my time but never one like you. You had me fooled all right. All that stuff about coming to Summerland to be a waitress . . . !" He clamped his knuckles against his hips and glared down at her. "Why couldn't you be

101

honest at least? Say you'd come at Archie's request?"

"What?" she squeaked and screwed up her face. Who had fed him this false information?

"Although I can see it might have been difficult," he conceded sarcastically. "He probably told you to keep your mouth shut. Investigating a rival concern is hardly something to shout your mouth off about. Archie never gives up does he? Won't be happy until he's seen a closure notice slapped on us. Well he's on to a loser this time. As for you!"

His tone threatened her. He stepped closer. She realized now they were quite alone as they stood near the cliff-edge. She remembered how Honey had hinted at Guy's involvement in Debbie's death. Her mind catapulted. What did she really know about this man? Only that he came from a peculiar family where his brother's behaviour was erratic and his father's vindictive.

One shove from him would send me

crashing to the beach, she thought. I've got to get away from him. The turmoil inside her made her jabber. "I didn't come to Summerland because Archie asked me. I'd never seen him before I came here. But if you must know, I'm the one who brought the state of these cliffs to his notice — and I presume it's what all this is about . . . " She'd been talking faster and faster and now she suddenly punched out at him.

It was like hitting a brick wall as her fists banged against his chest to push him out of her way. He snatched at her wrists and clamped his long fingers round them. At the same time the edge of the cliff gave way beneath her. Sand and gravel avalanched.

She screamed.

The way he snatched her towards him hurt her neck and shoulders. They both overbalanced. They rolled over and over, limbs locked. At last they came to a halt. Gasping she gazed up at him.

"Are you OK?" he said, breathing

heavily against her, his long legs still entwined around hers.

"You — you saved my life." Her voice was weak and shaky like the rest of her.

"If you'd gone over the edge you'd have taken us both. What in God's name made you punch out like that?"

She hesitated. A moment later she saw realization dawn in his eyes. They glittered diamond-bright and his voice came deeply, "Nil out of ten for judgement. You don't choose the right moments to be scared." There was an odd expression on his face. She felt his body pressure increase on hers and winced as his hard muscles dug into her.

"L-let me up!"

For a moment she thought he was going to refuse and her heart hammered but then he sprang to his feet. She stood up unsteadily and tried to regain her composure.

"Perhaps you can see now why I've been investigating these cliffs." Her voice betrayed her by shaking.

"You shouldn't have stood so close to the edge in the first place, should you?"

"Doesn't it bother you at all that your father's hotel could be sited on dangerous ground?"

"Doesn't it bother you that you could cause a great deal of worry to an old man, if he gets to hear about all this?

"I know you said you wanted to come up with something spectacular for your thesis but I'd say you were going over the top. There must be other ways you can distinguish yourself," he added contemptuously.

She gaped. Surely he didn't believe . . . ? But then he *was* quoting her. What was even worse was knowing there'd been a moment when it had excited her to think she might produce a piece of work that would impress everyone.

"All right then — if you don't believe me — believe the tell-tales!"

"Ah — the neat little row of pegs

you hammered in near the hotel," Guy muttered sarcastically.

"They prove the path there is creeping down the cliff because those pegs were in a perfectly straight line when I put them in but now the middle ones have moved . . . "

"Oh yes. Meant to tell you about that and apologise. I was slithering about on there with the dog and knocked them out. I put them back — obviously not quite in the same place." He shrugged.

She fumed inside. She knew he'd known exactly what he was doing. She might as well throw all her calculations away. Without speaking she turned and began to walk back to the camp but he strode beside her.

"There's really no need for all these investigations of yours, you know. Dad had his own done. Unbiased ones."

She didn't like his emphasis on the 'unbiased'. He continued "He had the foundations of the house strengthened and a report on general ground conditions. They were found to be adequate for what was needed. But if there's anything more you or Archie want to know, don't hesitate to ask," he added acidly.

"I will. Thank you," she said unsmiling. She was bewildered. Had she been on the wrong tack all along? If Cliff had already had a report . . .

But I must believe in my own judgement, she thought. I may not be qualified but I can suss out the situation using the knowledge I've got. If I'm wrong I make a fool of myself. So what? But the small frown on her face belied the reasoning.

"I'd be grateful if you didn't bring the subject up when you come for supper. My father's still not well and I don't want him concerned in any way."

"I'm not stupid," she murmured.

"I know."

She looked up quickly, surprised by the change in his tone. He nodded towards the chalets. "This is as far as I go."

"Who told you what I was doing?"

"Tracy told Neil."

"Tracy?"

"Didn't you know she's chasing my brother? Silly little girl doesn't know the first thing about him. For some reason she doesn't like you — seemed to think we should know what you were up to. She heard you and the boyfriend talking to her parents and told my brother."

"Neil was bothered about Dad finding out, and for once he took me into his confidence."

"And — and she told Neil Archie employed me simply to investigate the cliffs?" Her eyes were round with astonishment?

"Simple enough deduction. Archie's been waiting for years to . . . " He stopped and they both listened. There was a noise like someone sobbing. A figure came hobbling across the field towards them from the direction of the chalets. Alison thought she recognized Honey and as she came closer she ran towards her.

Honey's blouse was torn and hanging from her shoulder. One pendulous breast swung loose from its brief bra-cup.

"Honey!"

Honey gazed at them from under swollen eyelids. She stood like a child, arms hanging limply by her side as Alison put her own cardigan on her and buttoned it. Honey saw Guy standing behind Alison and turned her face away to try and hide it.

Then she fell to her knees and was sick. Afterwards she put her hands over her face and began to cry again.

"Who did this to you?" said Guy savagely.

"N'body," she muttered.

He put one hand round her to help her up. She sagged against him. He then slid his other arm under her legs and lifted her.

"Show me her chalet Alison."

"Not there! He's . . . " Honey gave up the struggle and rolled her head against Guy's broad chest.

★ ★ ★

The chalet was empty when they reached it. Whoever Honey was afraid of had left. Guy laid her on the bed while Alison squeezed a face-cloth under cold water and gently wiped the cut on Honey's face.

"Oh Hon. You've got to tell us who did it," she said.

"No no no . . ."

"OK," soothed Alison, stroking her hair.

"And tell *him* not to do anything either." Honey slid her gaze towards Guy, who seemed to fill the chalet.

"I'm only going to look outside." He opened the door. "If he's done it once he'll do it again." Honey sat up. "You'll cost me my bloody job."

"He punched you; that's obvious — tore your clothes and God knows what else. He . . . "

"I got away didn't I?" Honey was talking as if she'd got a plum in her mouth now. Her lip was swelling.

Alison said quietly, "The man's got to be found, Honey."

"Oh yes. And then what happens eh? He shops me." She glowered. "You know Archie. This place is advertized for families . . . " Tears filled her eyes and she held the cloth against her mouth. Suddenly she swung her legs to the ground. "Put the kettle on, eh, Ali? You might as well because I'm not leaving this chalet, not to go to the police and give statements or go to hospital or anything else.

"And you needn't worry. I got the bastard. I reckon I broke his little finger. Grabbed it and bent it back hard."

"I think you should get some rest," Guy said.

"You *are* going to do something, aren't you? I know your sort. You're the type who doesn't take any notice of what people say," gabbled Honey.

"No he won't. Not if you don't want him to. Will you?" Alison stared at Guy.

"Wanna bet?" Honey sounded cynical but anxious too.

Alison frowned. She knew Honey was right. He'd go straight to the police. She could see it in his eyes. She sat on the bed beside Honey. "Go on. Tell him."

After a pause, Honey mumbled, "My chalet number is one of the first that blokes get to know when they arrive. It's passed on, see. They know it before they get to know where the Arcade is, or the Games room — or anything."

"I see. Popular lady." His eyes were unblinking.

"You could say that. But . . . I don't take on marrieds!" She looked up. "I got my principles in spite of everything. I — I was married myself once."

"I didn't know that." Alison was surprised.

"Lot you don't know — like he beat

112

me up regular." She brought up her hand and stroked her cheek lightly. "Got one like him tonight didn't I? But this is nothing, I can tell you. I got worse than this from my husband."

"Where is he now?" said Alison softly.

"God knows. I don't, and I don't care either. I got a baby you know? He's with my mum. Nearly two he is. Brent's his name." She eyed them both. "I like to send extra money home. My mum's a widow. She hasn't got much."

Guy nodded and said softly, "It isn't worth getting it this way. You're at risk in too many ways."

"Yeah I know. But you see — if Archie finds out what I've been doing, that's me without a job. He's always on about what a respectable place this is."

There was a pause. "OK. If you really insist on nothing being done about this then I'll respect your wishes. But you're wrong! No woman should tolerate being abused by any man either mentally or physically. She's the same rights to consideration as he has."

His voice rose. "Look in the mirror, Honey. Say to yourself, NO ONE has the right to do this to my body and what's more I'm not going to let him do it to anyone else."

Honey said nothing but lowered her head. Guy left the chalet and Alison followed him.

"It sickens me!" he fumed. "He shouldn't get away with it."

"She must decide," she said quietly. She'd seen a different side to him that night. She added softly, "I'm glad you were with me when she needed help."

"She's got problems and she'll have even more if she goes on like this, whatever the reason."

"She's right about Archie. He wouldn't let her stay on if he knew."

"Highly moralistic is he? So what happened to morals when he sneaked you in to look for ways to have Dad's

114

hotel closed down?"

"You refuse to believe me, don't you? I really did come here as a waitress! When I told him I was studying geology and thought the place could be due for a landslip he gave me time off to investigate further."

"And you honestly don't believe he snapped up that information to use it to his own ends?"

"Yes."

"Yes you do, or yes you don't?"

"I believe he did. But that doesn't alter facts. It doesn't alter what I think about the cliffs."

"We talk about Archie being rigid — what about you? You could be wrong. Those cliffs have been like that for years. The buildings near them have stood the test of time. I told you Dad had his own engineer's report."

"I know, and that does make a difference." She frowned.

"And after all you aren't . . . "

"Qualified? I know!"

"I was going to say, you aren't a

woman who'll jump to conclusions until you've considered *all* aspects — without being influenced by Archie's dubious motives."

Her instincts told her he was a man she could trust — more than she could ever trust Archie. She could believe him when he said the hotel had been studied for safety aspects. He would never take risks with guests' lives. He was too compassionate. She'd seen that in the chalet just now.

She looked up as his hands touched her shoulders. Stars glimmered above him on a velvet sky. From a distance the disco slammed its vibrancy into the night air.

"You're ambitious Alison. You want to prove yourself don't you?"

His fingers moved against the back of her neck and she felt a prickling in the fine hairs there. She knew he was about to kiss her. Her back arched and her heart beat harder.

"Goodnight Alison," he whispered. And he walked away.

116

She stood alone trembling. Perhaps he didn't find her attractive after all? And yet she was certain . . .

You fool! said her brain. Don't you know he *wants* you to swoon over him just like Debbie did? Then you might abandon the project rather than displease him. You've just experienced an expert little seduction scene.

As Alison climbed into bed that night, Honey said, "I heard you two talking. Is it true Archie wants you to find out if the cliffs are dangerous? Why didn't you say that's why he gave you time off? Archie would be dead pleased if the hotel had to close."

"Please forget what you heard. Nothing's certain any more. I thought I was right about the movement of some pegs I knocked in but . . . oh, let's not talk about it!" She leaned on her elbow. "Are you sure you're OK Honey?"

"I wish I could forget how the swine went for me. Trouble is he's bust off a lump of my tooth. It feels like a dagger."

Alison sat bolt upright.

"What's up?" said Honey.

"I just remembered something! An old boat on the beach." She lay back again. "Tomorrow. I'll look tomorrow," she said wearily and closed her eyes.

There was a long silence before Honey murmured, "That Guy is really something else. I never knew he was so nice." A moment later she started to snore. But Alison was wide awake again.

The following morning was the start of the heat-wave.

After breakfast Alison sat with Honey in the ballroom.

"Don't you want to go and watch them pick Miss Beautiful Hands?" asked Honey dolefully, her mouth swollen and bruised.

Alison shook her head. She hadn't the least intention of leaving Honey alone.

A small boy ran across the caramel-coloured floor.

"My Brent wears little red shorts like

that." Honey sighed deeply.

"Is there anything you'd like to do today?" Alison breezed.

"I don't want to go where I'll hear any more comments like, 'Who've *you* been fighting with Honey?' I want to go where it's quiet. Like the island. That's it — the island! Maurice will let us borrow his boat."

Alison spotted Tracy at the far end of the room. She excused herself for a minute and hurried across to her.

"Yeah?" said Tracy sulkily.

Alison ordered herself to keep her cool. She wanted to clear the air with her — find out why she'd been making trouble.

Before she could speak, Tracy snapped, "Dad tells me he's asked you to help me with schoolwork? Well I'd like you to know I don't want any help from you or anybody else."

"There's no need to be so rude about it."

"My God, Tracy! What a miserable kid you are!" Honey's voice echoed from behind Alison.

Tracy slewed them a black look. "D'you think I'd be friends with anybody who tried to steal my boyfriend?"

"Heck, I was only swimming near him," Alison retorted.

"You were flirting. I saw you."

Honey stepped closer to Tracy. "If you're talking about who I think you are, then I wouldn't let your old man find out if I were you."

"And if I were *you*, I wouldn't let him find out about the little business you've got going on the side, because I don't reckon he'd like that, not one little bit."

"Let's go, Honey," murmured Alison.

Tracy looked at Alison and sneered, "I'm not surprised she's been done over. What happened? Did he want more than his money's worth? Her client?"

She'd barely got the words out when Honey hurled herself at Tracy, snatching at her hair. The two of them began kicking and scratching one another with the impact of all-in wrestlers.

"Stop it!" Alison shouted.

A group of startled campers turned and gaped.

Archie appeared from nowhere, his expression like thunder. He seized hold of both Honey and Tracy and yanked them apart. Dishevelled and breathing heavily, they glowered at one another. Archie shook them. "Marvellous! Bloody marvellous example! My daughter and a waitress fighting like a couple of alley-cats! Now, what the hell do you think you're both playing at?"

He saw the bruise on Honey's mouth and rapped out, "Did you do that, Trace?"

"No I didn't! It was one of her . . . " She stopped, still out of breath and caught the look on Honey's face. In that instant both girls knew they depended on one another's silence. Tracy mumbled sulkily, "No I didn't."

"Fine state of affairs! Look at the

two of you! And here's me and your mum going away for the weekend and thinking we can leave you to help run the place, Trace. Both of you go and get yourselves cleaned up!"

As they both slunk away, Alison saw Honey glance towards her and give a surreptitious grin, opening her hand behind her back. In it was a big clump of ginger-coloured hair.

★ ★ ★

When Alison went down to the beach it seemed to her the whole of Summerland must be sunbathing, swimming or playing there. She picked her way between tanned bodies and eventually reached the part of the beach in front of the hotel. She knew what she was looking for. She'd seen it the day before but it hadn't registered. Not until Honey spoke about her broken tooth did it occur to her it was an important piece of evidence for her thesis — and she'd missed it.

Fine geologist you're going to make, she told herself cynically.

She stopped when she reached the bow of the old boat, sunk in the sand. Yes, she was certain there was less of it on the surface. The greater part of it was now hidden by sand and gravel — sand and gravel that had not been there the first time she spotted it. Simon had agreed there were springs permeating through the cliff, softening it and causing parts of it to slide down to the beach. Now it was happening more often.

She gazed up the cliff-side with an anxious expression. But this time she told herself she wasn't charging off to report her findings to anyone, not even Simon. She'd use common sense this time; get her results properly tabulated first.

She pressed her lips together and looked up to where the pegs she'd knocked in had been dislodged, then she started to climb up to re-align them.

That afternoon she was poring over books in the chalet when Honey burst in.

"I don't know how you can sit here in all this heat. And anyway I thought we were going over to the island? Maurice'll lend us his boat."

"Have you been there before?" Alison looked up, pencil poised over her notebook.

"Course. We snuck over once to have a beach party. You'd like it."

* * *

Honey had just started the boat when they spotted Janet racing towards them.

"Hold it Hon! There's been an accident. Your mum phoned. It's Brent."

"What's up?"

"It's not serious — but you know what your mum's like. Rita says you can go home."

"Can I help?" Alison jumped from the boat as well.

"Only if you know how to stop my mum ringing up every time my Brent falls down and scratches himself. I got to go though. You go on to the island. You'll like it."

After Honey and Janet left, Alison hesitated, but after looking at the crowded beach and then towards the island with its towering lighthouse, she got back in the boat.

At the island she tied it to a jetty and padded over deep sand. On such a beautiful day it was hard to imagine this was a destructive coastline with storms wreaking havoc along its shore. But they didn't build the lighthouse for nothing she told herself, nor the fine modern one further along the coast leaving this one disused.

She clambered over rocks and stones and then began to climb steps to the tall grey building.

The entrance room held a stillness that startled her. It was much cooler in there, and she pulled on her sweater and gazed around the circular chamber.

More steps wound upwards.

She guessed the next level must have been the engine room. She rested her arms on a deep window-sill and gazed through the small window. A wide turquoise sea rocked gently for miles. The sight made her feel suddenly small and unimportant.

There was a noise that sounded like someone on the steps. But she hadn't seen a soul when she approached the lighthouse. Perhaps some visitors had arrived in the meantime?

She went to look but could only see a small beam of dusty sunshine dancing through the doorway.

But when she climbed to the next level she saw signs of someone having settled themselves down in there: upturned boxes covered by a rug, empty cans of drink — and there was an oddly sweet smell in there.

She sat on the box. The rug was warm. So she hadn't been mistaken? Someone else had been in the lighthouse with her — and they weren't closetted in there smoking ordinary cigarettes.

She felt apprehensive now. Suppose that person was still lurking in the place? She told herself her best bet was to get out — fast.

She breathed a sigh of relief when she reached the entrance again and saw no one, then she marched forthrightly out to the jetty.

She stood in the sunshine and laughed. No one there at all! Whoever had been in the lighthouse must have wanted to get away as quickly as she did. Then her expression changed. There was no sign of the boat either.

Then to her great dismay she spotted it half-way between the island and the mainland. All she could do now was to hope some holidaymakers would come out there and take her back with them.

She climbed back up the cliff steps. The sun was scorching. She clipped her dark silken hair into a top-knot for coolness and felt her legs starting to burn below her small white shorts. She found a spot near hawthorn bushes that was shady, and where she could look out from the clifftop and wave to any boat she saw.

She rested her elbows on her sweater on the ground and watched sea-birds dunking their beaks in a drifting sea.

I'm really lucky to have the chance to write a thesis about this lovely area and live here at the same time, she told herself. Fancy — I nearly gave up the opportunity when Mum died. Life has to go on . . . like the sea ebbing and flowing; sun rising and s . . . She lay back and closed her eyes.

She didn't know how long she'd been asleep when she woke to hear rustling in the bushes. She blinked and sat up, her pulse racing.

"Well! You're good at camouflaging yourself! I've been looking everywhere for you," said a deep voice.

She sprang to her feet, exclaimed "Guy!" and just stopped herself from falling into his arms with relief.

"Some bloke spoke to Neil on the beach — worried because he'd lent you his boat and you hadn't got back. He said you should have been in the dining-room. Anyway I wasn't doing anything and borrowed Neil's boat to come over here. Nice day for it. Hope it stays that way." He glanced towards the sea.

"I'm so pleased to see you!" she exclaimed.

"Heh, don't look so worried." Without warning he drew her towards him and caressed the nape of her neck. Her body seemed to melt against him.

She wondered if he could feel her heartbeat against his broad chest. "You're hungry?" he said.

"Very!"

"I grabbed a bit of food on the way out."

She demolished chicken drumsticks, granary bread — and champagne. Bubbles seemed to float into her head and explode. When she looked up he was watching her with an amused smile.

It made him look more attractive than ever. He was wearing a scarlet Lacoste T-shirt and cream pants. He sat with one knee crooked, his elbow resting on it as he held a glass of champagne. She noticed the dark hairs on his tanned arms and the Rolex watch round his wrist.

"So are you going to tell me what happened?" he said.

When she told him about her visit to the lighthouse he only shrugged.

"People aren't supposed to come over here but they do. It was probably a tramp — or kids from Summerland. We used . . . " He stopped as if thinking better of it, then said, "We'd better get back; looks like a mist coming down."

"Shall I show you the room with the boxes in it? There's a peculiar sme–"

"No point," he said quickly, almost abruptly. He stood up to leave and she followed, her legs feeling hollow. Her head was about clear enough for her to realize she wasn't herself. Guy helped her down the steps to the jetty and into Neil's boat. She knew he thought she hadn't tied up Maurice's securely. She was even beginning to wonder as much herself.

Neil's boat wouldn't start.

"Don't worry — won't take me long to fix it," he said. "In the meantime you'd better sit down . . . The champagne wasn't such a good idea."

By the time he'd got the boat started the mist had turned into a fog that enveloped the mainland. He looked out to sea, frowning.

"Well *I* think it was a lovely idea!" she piped. When he glanced at her with a puzzled expression she added, smiling, "The champagne."

"You haven't a clue what's happening." The corner of his mouth twitched.

"I have!"

"We're going to have to hang on a bit until this lot clears."

"I know," she remarked, ignoring the turmoil growing inside her; a longing . . . for what? she asked herself. Her stomach twisted when he touched her cheek lightly, his eyes gazing deeply into hers.

"Show me this room in the lighthouse then," he murmured.

5

GUY gripped Alison's hand as they walked back together. Her bones felt like egg-shells.

Inside its shroud, the island seemed to be disappearing. Waves slapped it while gulls cried plaintively.

As they approached the lonely lighthouse, she remembered what Honey had said about not getting involved with Guy. But wasn't that before Honey had got to know him better?

Alison stumbled as they climbed the rocky path and Guy caught her. But as soon as they entered the lower chamber of the lighthouse, he released her hand. Suddenly he seemed aloof. He glanced quickly about him. He spoke gruffly without looking at her.

"Put your sweater on."

"I'm warm enough."

"You won't be for long. Not in here."

There was a desolate emptiness about the place. Alison swung her sweater around her shoulders and tied the sleeves under her chin.

Guy's sudden cool and distant manner puzzled her. He had the look of a man who had entered an alien world, and yet he had been to the lighthouse before.

She dragged her feet as she followed him to the next level. Sometimes she wished she'd had more experience with men — enough to be able to sort out dreams from reality.

The only man she'd know really well was Simon, who had helped and encouraged her when life had been at its most bleak; Simon who had assumed they would marry. She felt a twinge of guilt. She owed Simon.

"Is this the room you were telling me about?" Guy said.

She pointed to the rug spread across

the boxes. "That was still warm when I sat on it."

"Probably kids messing around," said Guy.

"If so, they could have let my boat go simply for a laugh." The place seemed fairly normal to her, now.

"Possibly." She realized he was still deep in his own thoughts, and had been since entering the lighthouse.

"Shall we go and see the rest of the place?" She tried to sound bright but her head was still woolly.

"I haven't come for a guided tour."

Alison wanted to ask him why he had come. Instead she said stonily, "Perhaps it would be a better idea if we tried to make it back to the mainland after all."

"No way. There are tricky currents round here at the best of times but in this fog we'd be asking for trouble. We may as well make ourselves comfortable."

He pushed the boxes against the wall, sat at one end and indicated that

135

Alison sat beside him. She ignored him and pretended to examine the chamber. When she looked at him again, his eyes were closed, his arms folded, his long legs stretched out.

"You might as well. We could be here all night," he murmured.

"I'm not staying all night!" Alison declared.

"What are you going to do? Swim?"

She perched on the end of the boxes. She thought he'd fallen asleep, he was quiet for so long, but then he said, without opening his eyes, "This boyfriend of yours . . .

"Simon?"

"What does he do?"

"He's a geologist."

"Useful."

"What does that mean?"

"He can help you write your thesis on how to condemn our home."

Alison refused to rise to the bait. He continued, "Is it serious? You and him?"

"I — he — " She couldn't answer.

The doubt and confusion concerning Simon which she'd felt for a long time only added to the lightness in her head. Guy opened one eye sleepily. She heard herself gabbling.

"Simon has been wonderful to me. He's helped me a lot. He's a very, very kind person."

"Sounds like a good guy." He turned towards her. Now his deep blue eyes were fixed on her with a more gentle expression. "But gratitude is no substitute for love, is it? Or desire."

"I want . . . " she began hotly.

"What? What do you want?" Guy interrupted. "It's my guess you don't know. Correction — I don't think you'll admit to what you want. You might have done for a second, out there on the boat, but now . . . "

"It was you who changed! From the minute we came into the lighthouse you were like a different person."

"There you are — it just proves I'm an unsociable pig of a man."

He narrowed his eyes and grinned disarmingly, mimicking a gangster's drawl. "Well, we gotta make the best of things, kid, because there's only you and me here now."

In spite of everything, Alison felt a giggle rise in her throat. She decided she wasn't quite sober. Suddenly she jerked her head and listened. "What's that?"

"I didn't hear anything."

"I was sure . . ."

"Relax." He laid his large brown hand over her small one.

"But suppose there's someone lurking about?"

"Are you still scared? With me here?" His tone was jocular now. He'd dismissed whatever had been on his mind before.

So, she thought cynically, it was OK now, was it, to be all jolly and friendly again? She tried to draw her fingers away from his, but couldn't. She wondered if he could feel how her pulse was galloping? Her mouth

138

dried as he edged closer to her.

"Shall I tell you why you really wanted to come in here, Alison?"

"No . . . I . . . " She didn't finish the sentence. She tried to push him away but as his lips lingered on hers, her body melted.

"You don't love him you know," he murmured at last.

"How would *you* know how I feel?" she said breathlessly.

"Alison." His voice was like a caress.

"I shouldn't have come. It was a mistake," she said weakly.

"No. No mistake." He was whispering, kissing her cheeks, her hair, her neck.

Dreamlike, she felt his hands slide down her sweater. There were only the two of them in an intimate world of mists and dangerous currents. Only he could extinguish the fires that began to rage inside her.

She felt weightless as he laid her back on the rug. Her body was like a small drifting boat about to be crushed on the rocks. His lips bruised her but the taste of him was exquisite. Her body ached for him.

He suddenly released her, leaned back and put his finger to his lips.

"What's wrong, Guy?"

Alison heard someone call, "Is anybody there?"

★ ★ ★

Later, when she tried to think rationally about the interruption, all she could remember was how her body would not stop tingling.

The two tourists, who had got themselves stranded on the island, stayed to keep them company until the mist lifted.

It was in the early hours when Guy helped her out of the boat near the hotel. She saw Maurice's bobbing boat in the distance and ran along the beach. She waded into the sea towards it. Guy followed her.

"I'll teach you how to tie decent

knots . . . " he began, then stopped, frowning, as he examined the rope trailing from the boat. "This has been cut. If I were you, I'd stay away from the island."

Alison saw genuine concern in his face. As they walked back together he put his arm around her. She felt warm and protected. Her heart soared.

★ ★ ★

It was Archie's manager who brought her down to earth.

"Damn silly to go out there on your own. Everyone knows that stretch of water is lethal. It's bad enough Honey wasn't here without you going missing, making us even more short-handed."

"I'm sorry."

"You don't look sorry. As it happens, we were all worried about you."

That subdued Alison and she threw herself into work to make up for the time she'd missed.

She wondered when Guy would

contact her again.

Honey returned that evening. "Mum is so fussy. I knew Brent would be OK. Still — it was smashing to see him again . . . but Mum kept going on about my face. She didn't believe me when I said I'd walked into a door. She's seen it all before. So . . . what happened on the island?"

"I told you, those tourists came along and stayed with us."

"You go a funny colour when you talk about it."

"Probably because I've got a headache."

"Hangover. That's what that is!" Honey grinned. "So, when are you seeing Guy again?"

Alison adopted a casual attitude. "No idea. Oh . . . I am going to supper at the hotel next week." She frowned. "The trouble is, I've nothing decent to wear."

"None of my clothes would fit you, but, if you like, I can show you a place where you can buy great stuff.

142

Designer clothes and everythin'."

"I can't afford designer clothes, Honey!"

"Don't worry. Leave it to me."

★ ★ ★

Friday night was balloons and fancy-dress but Alison found it difficult to get into the festive spirit. She'd been so sure Guy would have contacted her.

Honey's fancy-dress was a mask that concealed a developing black eye. She shouted above the thumping disco. "I'm not staying long. Not with Tracy showing off all night. Anyway, it's too hot for dancing."

Jack shouted back, "You know where Archie and Rita have gone?"

"Yeah. They're visiting some fabulous holiday chalet hotel at Hopton-on-Sea — being wined and dined for the weekend, lucky things. I expect Archie's gone to pinch ideas. I reckon there are going to be big changes round here."

"I hate change. We're all right as we are," moaned Jack.

"Well, if he smartens up the place and makes it all modern, he won't go for amateur entertainment like you. He'll want the big names then. You and your guitar . . . "

Honey stopped and leapt from her chair when one of the staff asked her to dance.

Left alone with Jack, Alison felt sorry for him. "Big names cost money, Jack."

"Oh, I'm not worried. I won't be losing *my* job! Archie's known me too long. I worked for him when he had a shop. He knows who his friends are."

Alison found it uncomfortably hot in the room. She wondered what on earth had possessed her to come as Neptune's daughter. Her hair was thick and heavy enough without seaweed twined in it!

She moved towards one of the open doors for some fresh air and spotted a figure she thought she recognized. Her pulse went full gallop — until she realized the tall dark man wearing a mask was not Guy.

Tracy raced past her and spoke excitedly to him. "I *knew* you'd come! I knew!" Her eyes were shining.

"I've only come to see what goes on here. My God, the place is jumping."

"I know. Great isn't it? Dance with me, Neil."

"I'm gasping for a drink."

"I'll get you one! Don't go away!"

After Tracy had rushed off, Neil flipped up his mask and winked at Alison. "Her old man *is* away for the weekend, isn't he?"

"You're crazy. Someone is going to recognize you and tell him."

"Not if I keep this mask on, little mermaid."

Alison fancied his hands shook slightly as he readjusted the mask. He grinned. "This is the sort of dancing we should have at the hotel. We need a bit more life — bit more fun for the kids. I want to have a good look round this place."

"Have you just come to pinch ideas?"

"Could be."

She wondered how much he'd drunk already when he partnered Tracy on the dance floor and began larking around and calling out silly remarks. Some of the older guests looked on disapprovingly, but Tracy laughed hysterically at his antics.

It had been announced earlier that the speciality act had failed to turn up and there was a last minute surprise item. As the dancing finished and everyone sat down, Alison was agog with curiosity.

The first bars of 'One Singular Sensation' brought an attractively dressed woman wearing sequinned midnight-blue on to the floor. She flourished a chiffon scarf and sank into a low curtsey. As the spotlight swept over her the crowd gasped as they recognized Maurice.

146

There was a burst of applause. With a cheeky grin, Maurice launched into a raucous rendering of 'There Is Nothing Like A Dame'. He was such a roaring success, Alison wondered later why he hadn't left it at that instead of cavorting between tables flicking his scarf provocatively at the men and finishing up sitting on Neil's lap.

Everyone laughed — except Neil. He jerked his elbows back then thrust his arms forward, giving Maurice a push that propelled the slight figure along the shiny floor. Maurice sat up, pulling a comical face and rubbing his head, as if the whole incident were part of the clowning act.

But Neil wasn't finished. With his face contorted, he marched across to Maurice and dragged him up by his shoulder straps. It was the crowd hissing and booing that made him let go and stride angrily to the door, with Tracy in anxious pursuit.

As Honey and Alison were leaving, Honey said, "Only a bit of fun, wasn't it? No need for that guy to have a go at Maurice — and I can guess who it was, too!" She wiped her forehead. "It's so hot. Why don't we go for a swim?"

"At this time of night?"

"I've wanted to have a swim all day," sighed Honey.

"Why didn't you?"

"And let everybody see my bruises? You must be kiddin'."

"OK. Let's get our cossies."

"No need for cossies. No one will see us in the dark."

★ ★ ★

Had Alison realized it was such a magical experience swimming in the nude, she would have done it before. Waves slapped silkily against her soft skin as she splashed happily, making fluorescent tracers with her fingers.

"This is marvellous!"

"Told you." Honey's voice came from the distance.

"Where are you? I can't see you."

"Over here."

Alison saw phosphorescent sparks in the direction of her voice. She relaxed and glided lazily on her back in the inky water.

Suddenly she heard a soft splashing near her. The next minute Guy rose from the water beside her like a magnificent Poseidon. She gasped.

"Seems we all had the same idea," he said softly with wry amusement.

Alison stared. She had never seen such a body. And she had never felt so vulnerable.

"My God, you're beautiful Alison," he whispered, moving even closer. She was too startled and dumbstruck to get any words out, but she pressed her hands against his massive shoulders to push him away as he circled her with his arms like a steel girdle.

"Don't . . . " she began, but his mouth was over hers to silence her and she was locked hard against him. She was trembling under the power that grew in his rocklike limbs as they stiffened against her and she became weak and unresisting.

The sea sucked persistently, trying to force a channel between them.

He released her as suddenly as he'd appeared, diving under the water and striking out for the shore. Alison staggered from the impact of him, blood coursing round her body.

"Heh! Why didn't you answer me?" Honey had swam to her side.

"I — I didn't hear you." Alison felt out of breath.

"You OK?"

"Fine!"

"Ready to get out?"

"Not yet . . . In a minute."

A few minutes later as they walked along the beach, Alison asked, "Has Guy Kington really been around so much?"

"You mean, has he had a lot of women? I'll say. He's not the type to settle down with one. I've told you, don't raise your hopes in that direction . . . Heh! Listen!"

From the direction of Archie's little boat-shed they heard Tracy's voice followed by Neil's.

"What's the matter, Neil? Aren't I good enough for you or something?"

"Just clear off and leave me alone!"

Honey whispered, "She don't never learn."

Alison glanced over her shoulders. In the distance she could see the lights twinkling on the pier at Larborough. So much glitz and glitter. But how many seaside romances would collapse like sand-castles when the summer was over? In spite of what Honey had said about Guy, she was sure theirs would not be one of them.

* * *

When Archie and Rita returned from Hopton, he was like a fire-cracker waiting to be lit.

"I got these great ideas! Great ideas!" he enthused at the party he gave for

151

Rita's birthday. He called out, "I give you all — Summerland Camp! — except it ain't going to be called that any more." He paused to enjoy the curiosity he'd aroused.

"Are you going to expand, boss?" asked Jack hesitantly.

"Why must everybody talk about expansion? It isn't always the best way, not in today's climate, Jack."

"But I thought . . . "

"Look Jack, there's owners of holiday centres who're de-bedding. Do you know that?"

Jack looked perplexed. Archie chewed a sweet. "It's *quality* I want. Exciting developments — that's the secret. We provide facilities that keep our guests so happy they don't want — or need — to go abroad. There'll be everything here, indoors and outdoors. New exciting facilities. Get it?"

Alison saw doubts on Jack's face.

"Wh-where's that going to leave me, Archie?"

"Exactly where you want to be, Jack.

152

Exactly where you want to be. It's up to you. But we've all got to move with the times."

Archie's eyes glazed over. He opened his arms wide. "Summerland Holiday World. I can see it now."

But he didn't see Rita join the group.

"Is he telling you about the magnificent Chalet-Hotel complex we've just visited? Oh, we had ever such a smashing time. The director there was ever so kind and showed us . . ."

"I did have a few ideas of my own before we went there," pronounced Archie.

"Oh, there was everything there, wasn't there, Archie? Snooker, clay-pigeon shooting, badminton, indoor bowls . . . "

"I shall have all that. And de luxe chalets with tel–"

"And swimming-pools . . . "

"I shall have an indoor swimming-pool . . . "

"Fitness studio . . . "

"I didn't know you were keen on sport," cut in Archie testily.

"Flexible meal times . . . "

"Rit!" Archie scowled.

Rita glanced at her husband then drifted off into the room. Alison followed her.

"You really enjoyed the weekend, didn't you, Rita?"

"Oh, I did! I can't wait for Archie to start alterations here."

"I expect there'll be a lot of new buildings."

"Oh, there will be — to house all the lovely new facilities." She added on a whisper of excitement, her eyes dancing, "I've got a few ideas of my own."

And I bet Archie knows nothing about those, thought Alison.

★ ★ ★

Later that week, Alison and Honey took a train to Larborough.

Honey showed her the second-hand

charity shop where clothes were packed on free-standing rails.

"You'll find some good stuff in this lot, Ali. Women sometimes bring in frocks they've only worn once. They want to get their hands on some extra bread without the old man knowing. Look for designer labels."

"If they bring in clothes with designer labels, they can't be short of money."

"Don't you believe it. Some guys like their wives to be totally dependent on them for everything. Look at Archie. He loves being Mr Big, don't he? Poor old Rita relies on him for everything. He doesn't like her doing anything on her own. He was the same with his first wife."

"I didn't know Archie had been married before."

Alison searched through the rails. Then she spotted a jade dress hanging against the wall. A plump motherly assistant smiled at her.

"That's only just this minute come in. It's really classy."

Alison slipped into the tiny changing-room behind a curtain. She unzipped the beautiful jade dress and allowed the fine material to float over her head. One glance in the mirror told her she looked good. The cut of the material was superb. It emphasized her slim waist and softly rounded hips. It was dim in the little changing-room and she stepped outside to look in the shop mirror.

"Oh! It looks lovely on you!" the assistant beamed.

"I think it needs to be shortened, but I can soon do that."

Honey was open-mouthed. "That colour don't half suit you."

"Ever done any modelling, dear?" asked the assistant. Alison shook her head. Suddenly the thought of her evening at Cliff's Hotel was becoming more appealing.

Afterwards, while Honey shopped, Alison went to the library. She pored over copies of old newspapers, researching flooding and erosion in the area.

She was reading about sea-walls and their need to withstand extreme tidal conditions when her eyes caught the headline — DEATH PLUNGE FROM LIGHTHOUSE."

She snatched up the paper and read on: — 'Eighteen-year-old Deborah Sheperd crashed to her death on jagged rocks pounded by waves.

'I saw her jump,' said 19-year-old boyfriend Guy Kington, playboy son of Cliff's Hotel owner.

Alison sat motionless, staring at the print. She stood up and walked to the reception desk.

"Could I please see later editions of this newspaper?"

A few moments later, a librarian padded to her table and laid a pile of papers on it.

★ ★ ★

On the way back to Summerland, Alison was engrossed in her thoughts and scarcely heard Honey chattering

157

about her shopping expedition.

It looked as if the police had been suspicious of Guy's involvement in the affair, but it seemed there had not been enough evidence to accuse him of anything.

Archie's vitriolic rantings had been quoted at length. "Two spoilt brats of that hotel owner . . . My Debbie — an innocent young girl who would never have taken to drugs of her own free will, besotted by Guy Kington who used his power over her. No! We didn't know our daughter was pregnant. If it takes for ever, I'll get even with the whole Kington family . . . "

The phrases swirled in Alison's head. She glanced at Honey and saw she'd nodded off to sleep.

She wondered if Debbie had been racing to get away from Guy when she landed up in the gallery of the lighthouse? If so, why?

She remembered how Guy had been with her in there. What would have happened if she'd resisted his advances?

He was a pretty determined character. Suppose *she* had run away? She gave a start as Honey snored.

Alison ran her fingers through her hair. What on earth was she thinking of? Guy would never hurt anyone. Hadn't he saved her from toppling over the cliff?

But one of Archie's remarks rang true. There was no doubt Guy did have a strange power over women. She'd seen how they reacted when he smiled that slow seductive smile . . . the way she herself had reacted.

But by the time they got back, Alison had devised a dozen alibis for Guy. She'd also managed to convince herself their relationship was nothing like the one he'd had with Debbie.

He loves me. I'm sure he does, she repeated to herself. She frowned and bit her lip. She had read something else in the library that troubled her — about erosion. The facts matched up to a lecture she'd heard at college and had been trying to remember.

A set of circumstances that could lead to a full-scale disaster.

Should she disregard them? Tell herself she could be mistaken? It would make life easier. If she brought them to light she could say goodbye to any relationship between her and Guy . . . but wasn't it her job to dig out the truth?

"You look worried. And you just bought yourself a lovely new dress, too," said Honey.

Alison gave a determined nod. "Yes! And I'm going to enjoy myself in it! And I'm going to forget about my stupid old thesis!"

"I'll tell you this much. When you get to the hotel in that frock, you'll knock 'em sideways."

But neither of them were to know that fate was about to play one of its dirty tricks on Alison.

6

ALISON tingled with excitement as she approached Cliff's hotel, where she was to be a supper guest. Guy had never seen her dressed up.

She resisted an urge to skip up the steps to the veranda; she wanted to maintain the new sophisticated image. The original owner of the beautiful jade dress she was wearing, would never have skipped up steps.

"Ah. Good evening — Alison." Cliff hobbled with his stick across the vestibule. She knew he'd nearly forgotten her name.

When Guy suddenly appeared from the lounge, her heart raced.

"Looks as if it's going to be a pleasurable evening, eh, Guy?" Cliff slid his son a foxy glance. Guy's dark dinner jacket lay sleek across his wide shoulders. His white shirt was luminous against his bronze skin.

His cool hands enfolded hers. "You look nearly as good as the last time we met."

Colour swamped her cheeks as she remembered the midnight swim and she quickly averted his gaze.

"That's not a very gallant remark," Cliff said as they went to the bar lounge with its comfortable green leather armchairs. "There's a world of difference between Alison's waitress's uniform and that expensive-looking dress. I must change my ideas about staff at holiday camps being poorly paid."

"Not camps any more, Dad. They're called centres now, or holiday parks . . . "

"Huh! As far as I'm concerned, that place across the road is a camp, and one up from tents."

"You wouldn't say that if you'd been there." Guy smiled wryly.

"Good God. Don't tell me *you* have?"

"Sure."

"Then you must be out of your mind, that's all I can say."

Cliff fell into a stony silence while Guy ordered drinks.

Alison noted Guy's self-possessed manner. This was not a man who would be afraid of a confrontation with Archie, but he *would* be wary of the publicity such a meeting might provoke, with any subsequent damage to the hotel's business.

As she sipped her Martini, Alison became aware of his sensual gaze sweeping her body.

"That dress," Cliff said, stroking his chin. "I'm sure I've seen . . . "

"I suggest we go on to the dining-room," interrupted Guy.

They sat at a table set for five, near a window. Outside, lawns and rockeries tumbled towards a shiny wrinkled sea.

I bet Archie would like to see this lot, thought Alison. The room was like a crystal palace with glittering chandeliers and twinkling glass and cutlery that must have been polished for hours!

"This is a beautiful room, Mr Kington," she enthused.

"I hope you find the menu to your liking too. Big change from that camp, eh? Don't suppose you get much of a choice there?

"As a matter of fact, the meals are pretty good," she said.

Cliff grunted. He glanced towards one of the doors. "Where the hell is Neil? Oh . . . and about time too."

Alison's jaw dropped when she spotted Neil. With Kedrun.

Kedrun's wide eyes encompassed the men as they stood up. She pouted poppy-moist lips. "I'm sorry if we're late," she crooned.

"Not a bit, my dear. You aren't at all. Let me see, you two ladies know one another, don't you?" Cliff's gaze slanted from Kedrun to Alison before realization flooded his eyes. "Of course! I know where I've seen that colour before!" He stared at Alison's jade dress. Their looks told her all she needed to know.

"Let's order, Dad," said Guy brusquely.

Alison did not have her usual hearty appetite, although the meal was perfect for a summer evening, from the fresh salmon to the creamy tangerine charlotte. Neil knew how to get the best out of his staff. How different he appeared this evening to the time she had seen him at the dance. He was a man of many moods, she thought.

Tact hung over the table like mist over the island. The conversation had been directed at every topic except clothes.

Kedrun had been too well bred to do more than raise a carefully pencilled eyebrow when she saw Alison's dress. Kedrun herself was wearing a slim black tube of a gown. It showed off her shiny blonde hair to perfection. It glittered as she talked animatedly to Guy.

It's ridiculous to ruin my appetite

165

because of a little thing like pride, Alison thought. So, what if she was wearing Kedrun's dress? It was simply an unfortunate stroke of fate and she had to make the best of it.

"Did you enjoy the meal?" asked Guy.

"It was delicious. Really lovely."

"And you — you look really lovely."

His lingering stare made her blush as he took in the sight of her thick raven hair licking at the snug-fitting bodice.

She said brightly, "I had to take up the hem. It originally belonged to a taller lady." Her voice faltered slightly. "But you know that, of course."

Alison realized Kedrun was watching them both with a frown playing on her smooth aristocratic forehead. That frown spelt trouble.

Kedrun's voice rang out loud and clear. "I hear you are investigating the state of the cliffs?" she said to Alison.

"What cliffs?" Cliff was immediately alerted.

"More wine anyone?" Guy beckoned a waiter.

"What part of the cliffs?" His father's steely eyes were pinned on her. Guy threw her a warning look. Kedrun saw it. Although she had wanted to make things awkward for Alison, she had not intended to displease Guy and now tried to make amends by changing the topic of conversation entirely.

"How far have you got with your new book, Guy?"

"I'm working on . . . "

"Alison?" Cliff now sounded peeved.

"It's a thesis I'm doing for college, Mr Kington. That's all. I'm studying the coastline."

"The coastline near my hotel?"

She nodded.

"Why the interest? Why this area?"

Alison wet her lips. She glanced around at happy chattering guests; men, women, children who might fall into a deep contented sleep one night after a sandy sun-soaked day, unaware that the weather was about to change for the worst. Unaware of gales that could occur when tides were at spring.

How she had wanted to put all such thoughts behind her, especially that night, but it was useless. Before leaving the chalet she had heard on the news about cliffs crumbling in a coastal town in the southeast. How clay at the foot of the cliffs had eroded, leaving no support for sandstone above. The district council had declared houses within fifty feet of the cliff-edge, unsafe.

Her mind had switched to similar calculations as she worked out the distance between Clifford's hotel and the edge of the cliff.

"Why?" he repeated doggedly.

"It's a very interesting area geologically and . . . and . . . " They were staring at her. "And I believe the cliffs in front of the hotel are on the move." She had not meant the statement to come out in such a staccato way. The silence that followed it screamed at her.

Cliff's face grew pink and puffy. "I've never heard such rubbish — if you'll forgive me saying so. Good God!" He laughed, except it did not sound like a laugh. "Those cliffs have been there for ever. They aren't suddenly going to take off and scuttle down the beach!" He ran his fingers through the air like a spider.

"Not a topic for discussion now," Guy said, frowning.

Neil stood up and signalled to the band assembled on a dais beside the dance floor.

Cliff leaned towards Alison. "I'm hardly stupid enough to have spent hard cash improving the hotel without getting a survey done first, my dear. And my reports from *experts* are sound enough, as for the land . . . " He stopped his carefully modulated argument to scowl at Neil. "For heaven's sake, sit down, boy!"

Alison saw the colour rise in Neil's cheeks. In an almost defiant gesture, he dragged his chair away from the table.

"It's about time we livened this place up a bit!" He snaked between couples starting to dance a slow foxtrot. He spoke to the band leader and the music trailed away. Seconds later, a livelier, much noisier rhythm filled the room.

Cliff screwed up his face as if he felt pain, but the dancers, in all their finery, began to jig about, laughing.

Neil returned to the table and held out his palms. "See, they like it!"

His father rose from his chair unsteadily and spoke through clenched teeth. "If you think, for one minute, I'm going to see this hotel turned into a cheap low-class . . . "

Guy said quietly, "I'd let this one go, Dad. They all seem to be enjoying themselves."

Cliff glared at Neil. "How much have you had to drink tonight?"

"I . . . "

"Don't tell me. I can guess."

"No one has had too much to drink, Dad. This sort of dancing can be great fun," said Guy, in a lighter tone.

"Not to me it's not. And one thing is certain. I don't have to stay here and be deafened."

He limped away, holding tightly on to his stick.

Guy read Alison's thoughts. "He's best left alone when he's like this."

Neil rounded on Guy. "Why do you have to interfere between him and me? We managed to sort out our own problems before you decided to come home on your — extended holiday! And sure as hell, we'll manage when you disappear again!"

"Can't we all go and dance?" said Kedrun nervously.

"I'd like to," agreed Alison quickly.

"It isn't the first time, is it big brother? In fact I can't remember a time when you didn't try to play God . . . " As Neil ranted on, Alison watched in astonishment that his father's reprimand could bring about such a swing in Neil's mood.

Guy stood up. "Leave it, Neil."

He turned to Alison, but Neil put a

claw-like hand on his shoulder. "You leave it! And leave us. The old man isn't ill any more. That's why you came home, wasn't it? Or was it to make sure he'd forgiven you? Not left you out of his will?" He was shouting. The music beat loudly. Guy remained silent and stony-faced.

"Let's dance." Guy put out his hand to Alison.

Neil clenched his fists. "This hotel is *mine*! Why don't you bugger off back to Greece?"

Alison felt Guy almost pushing her towards the dance floor. Neil's outburst was utterly bewildering to her. And why hadn't Guy stood up to him?

After they had been dancing a while, Guy looked down at her. "What's wrong?"

"Nothing."

"Don't lie."

"All right. If you must know — I can't understand why you let Neil talk to you like he did."

"Forget it," he said firmly.

"It isn't . . . "

"I said forget it!"

She did not like his tone. Whatever had been going on in this family, it did not give him cause to speak to her so abruptly. She drew in her breath. "Sometimes you sound, and behave, like your father."

"And sometimes you behave like a child."

"You didn't appear to think there was anything childish about me last night!"

"That was being mature, was it? Plunging naked into the sea where I was bathing and then playing hard to get . . . "

"And is that what Debbie did? Play hard to get?" The words were out before she could stop herself. Her anger gave way to alarm.

He stood quite still. His hands gripped her upper arms. His eyes splintered. Alison swallowed and felt her stomach tighten under his ferocious expression.

Why didn't he speak? Bawl her out, or something? she thought miserably.

"Guy, I . . . "

"Don't *ever* mention Debbie's name to me again!" There was stone — cold control in his voice.

"I'm . . . I'm sorry, Guy."

"And, while we're at it, there is something else you should know about me. I won't tolerate you, or anyone else, trying to interfere between me and any member of my family. Got it?"

Alison knew now that he regarded her as a rank outsider. She nodded dumbly.

Guy continued, "Then we understand one another. Now we'll forget it and dance again."

She blinked in amazement. Sure, she regretted her remark about Debbie — but that didn't mean she was going to dance to order! She glanced towards their table. Kedrun was sitting alone. Kedrun, who Guy had said, would *not* be coming!

"Why don't you ask Kedrun to

dance?" she said stiffly.

He looked towards Kedrun then his eyes scanned the room. "Where the devil has Neil got to, now? Excuse me a moment."

Alison returned to the table to collect her bag. Kedrun fingered her glass of tequila. "Well, this has turned out to be a deadly evening. Neil has vanished, Guy looks thunderous and . . . "

"And I'm wearing your dress." Alison shrugged and gave a sheepish grin.

"It suits you. I thought so when I passed the shop window."

"When you . . . ?"

"Shortly after I took the dress in." She went on smoothly, "I wasn't to know you would wear it tonight, was I?"

"No Kedrun, you weren't to know that," Alison agreed quietly.

"Yes, a most peculiar evening. When Neil asked me to come at the last minute, I had an idea he was trying to bring Guy and me together again, but after his little display, I can't imagine him doing anything to please big brother. Poor Guy.”

“ ‘Poor Guy’ looks as if he is coming to ask you to dance,” said Alison and went to find Cliff to say goodnight.

★ ★ ★

Cliff’s room was a sumptuous fusion of crimson and leather. He sat in a high-backed chair smoking a cigar.

“I hope Neil has apologized for . . . ”

“I’m afraid I must go, Mr Kington. But thank you for a lovely evening,” she said politely.

“You aren’t letting a family tiff drive you away, are you?”

“Of course not.” Alison had to sound as sincere as possible.

“That’s all it was, a family tiff. Not a bad way of clearing the air, really.”

Alison had her doubts about that. His remarks to Neil had acted like a trigger, releasing strange pent-up emotions in his son. Cliff bowed his shoulders and sighed.

"Perhaps he's right and I'm old-fashioned. Perhaps it's time for the old to give way to the new. Let the young ones have the reins." The corners of his mouth became ragged. "But it isn't in my hands any longer." There was a pause before he continued sadly, "I don't have much more time left for this world."

"You mustn't say that, Mr Kington!"

"I'm a sick old man, my dear. It's foolish of me to allow myself to get so stressed. One of these days it will kill me."

"I'm sure Neil and Guy . . . "

"Neil and I might have our disagreements, but he's a good son. He's stood by me." He raised his eyes to her. They were red-rimmed. "He'll miss me when I'm gone."

Alison crouched at his side. "They would *both* miss you. But you aren't going to die!"

He patted her hair. "I didn't mean to upset you. Now — no more talk about me. Tell me more about you.

Tell me about your project."

She stood up. "I don't think . . . "

"Go on. I'm very interested in what you said. These cliffs, now, you really believe they are dangerous, Alison?"

"Well . . . "

"Suppose I hold myself responsible for putting up more signs telling the public not to go too close; more fences, eh? Areas deemed out of bounds. That is the very least . . . " he clamped his hand to his chest.

"Mr Kington? What is it?" Alison dropped her bag.

"Tab . . . tablets — on coffee table . . . " he gasped.

Her hands were shaking as she handed him the box of tiny tablets. She rushed out to find Guy, who was dancing with Kedrun.

"I'm fine now! I'm fine. Don't fuss. You know how I hate fuss," she heard Cliff say as she stood outside his room with Kedrun.

"I'll get the doctor, anyway," said Guy.

"Don't want him. I want Neil."

Guy left the room and spoke to Alison. "God knows where Neil is. I'm calling for the GP."

"Would you like me to stay with your father?"

His look of gratitude gave a sudden lift to her feelings which only a moment before, in his father's room, had become tangled in a cat's cradle of emotions.

How could she present her evidence about the cliffs to the authorities and start something that would stress the old man even further?

★ ★ ★

The following day, Alison stood behind the hotel, staring down at the tell-tales. They had moved again. Guy would not have touched them this time. She was sure about that.

She walked slowly along the cliffs, looking out across a shimmering glass-topped sea. A tiny breeze brought the gritty smell of mussels and stringy seaweed. Bare-bottomed toddlers were splashing in glittering pools between the sun bathers.

She wondered how many of these beach-happy holidaymakers were staying at the hotel. She gave a quick shrug. Cliff had had a survey — he'd said so.

But conditions change, and you know it, she told herself.

She reminded herself sharply that she was simply writing a thesis . . . not putting herself forward as a supreme authority!

★ ★ ★

When Alison knew Simon was coming to see her, she made up her mind to tell him she could never marry him. She wished with all her heart that she were in love with him. Life without Simon would be an empty place.

She was alone in the chalet when he arrived. He seemed ill at ease. She wasn't feeling so easy herself. They both spoke at the same time. They laughed awkwardly. He kissed her, then Alison sat on Honey's bed with her hands clasped between her knees. He stuffed his hands in his pockets and gazed out of the window.

"I . . . er . . . I'm going away, Alison."

"Oh?"

"The Netherlands."

"Oh. Not far." She added brightly, "Netherlands — Pleistocene sands. Are you . . . ?"

"I won't be going alone." He turned, his cheeks pink.

"I see."

"I had to come and tell you. It was only fair."

She wondered why her stomach knotted. If he meant what she thought, it was a surprise, but surely it solved everything. He continued hesitantly, "I met Renate on a trip to Germany. I — I think I once mentioned her. She was just a friend, then. We corresponded and, well, somewhere along the line the

181

relationship changed. She came over to this country and I helped to get her a job in the department."

Alison swallowed. So no explanations were needed on her side after all? Simon loosened his tie.

"I'm sorry. But, you know, I've had the feeling things haven't been the same between us since you came to work in this damned awful place."

"It's a nice place." She managed lightness.

"You were hardly responsive the last time I came to see you."

"Were you seeing Renate, then?"

"Have you ever been truly in love with me? Like I was with you?" He leaned towards her, his forehead creased.

"I don't know, Si. I don't know. I wish I did," she said dully. She suddenly realized she might never see him again. She touched his arm as he sat opposite her. "Has it all been my fault, Si?"

He flushed again and started

stammering that it hadn't. Of course not. And she knew for certain, he'd been seeing Renate for much longer then he admitted. It was then that her pride took a dive.

"I came for another reason, too," he said as if happy to change the subject. "I've been talking to the guys at work about these cliffs. They were all keen to contribute." He unrolled a large sheet of paper and spread it out. He pointed to the diagrams he had drawn, showing areas of weakness.

"We all reckon you are on to something here. Some of the coastal towns used to be inland years ago, as you know, and the hotel you told me about on the crumbling headland . . . "

"They had a survey done."

"Date?"

"I don't know, but . . . "

"For heaven's sake, Ali!"

"I know; I know! I'll find out."

"I reckon they're in trouble. During the last war, a hotel near here went over the cliff. Tell them about that."

"No . . . I . . . "

"What's wrong?"

"There's a very sick old man there . . . I mean, houses, hotels — they've been here for years. Perhaps we're looking for trouble where there isn't any."

"I've not heard so much unprofessional clap-trap for ages." He frowned. "You've got yourself involved with the family who owns it, haven't you? Pity. Everyone I've spoken to thinks you could come up with a brilliant thesis."

"Damn the thesis! Guy . . . " she stopped.

He stared at her. There was a long pause before he spoke again. "And you let me go on about Renate! You are more interested in this Guy what's-his-name, than you ever were about me, aren't you?"

"Simon, when I knew you were coming to see me, I'd decided to tell you I couldn't marry you. But it has nothing to do with Guy Kington.

Like you, I've thought for a long time, things haven't been the same between us. But that doesn't mean I'm not going to miss you. Dreadfully." She gazed about her despondently.

"D'you know what I think? I think you don't *want* us to be right about the cliffs. I warned you not to let relationships get in the way. Does he love you?"

She shook her head.

"Then I suggest you get yourself down to earth again; back to work. Proper work! Or are you hell-bent on giving up what could be a tremendous career? Never mind this Guy person. Or some doddering old man who's got your conscience working overtime.

"You know, it's what I admire most about Renate. She never lets emotions get in the way. She's a scientist to her fingertips . . . as I once thought you were."

"I'm sure you'll both be ever so happy." She couldn't stop the trace of cynicism creeping into her voice. She was not prepared for what Simon did next. He bent low so his face was close to hers and whispered, "The stupid idiotic thing is that I suddenly want to make love to you." His hand cupped her breast.

"Si . . . !"

"Don't worry. I won't. Goodbye, Lissy. Good luck." He stopped at the door. "I want to see your boss before I leave. Unless . . . unless you'd like me to stay here a little longer — for old time's sake? We don't have to part like this."

"Goodbye Simon," she breathed.

The nick-name had brought back memories of college days. Of Simon and her. Together. Now he'd gone and a chapter had ended. Her feelings were a tangle of contradiction. She bent her head. She didn't hear Honey come in.

"Cheer up. They aren't bleeping well worth it, Ali."

"I feel as if I'd lost an arm or something."

"Last straw, eh?"

"Yup."

"Haven't seen you so fed up since you came here. You haven't been the same since the supper-do."

"I don't know what's wrong with me."

"Men! That's what's wrong with all of us. How about keeping me company in the bar?"

"Not tonight, thanks, Honey."

"OK, then we'll forget the whole lot of 'em in another way."

"That would be nice," Alison said glumly.

Honey glanced at Alison thoughtfully, then she said quietly, "You and me . . . we're friends, aren't we? Good friends?"

"Yes," said Alison, puzzled by her earnest tone.

"Then I can trust you. See, I want to do something for you, for a change. Make you feel better." She shut the door and turned the key; she closed the window.

187

Alison wafted the bodice of her blouse, "It's hot . . . "

"That won't worry you. Not in a minute."

"Wh-what are you talking about, Honey?"

"I'm talking about giving ourselves a buzz. OK?"

Alison stared as Honey took a small package out of her shoulder-bag. "You don't need to inject. Just a sniff. Once won't hurt you, and you'll forget your worries."

Alison gaped. She couldn't believe what Honey was suggesting.

"Go on!" Honey jerked her wrist with the packet in her hand.

"Do you know what that stuff does to you?" Alison croaked, after a dumbfounded silence.

"You the expert, then?" Honey stiffened.

"I know someone at college who screwed up his life like that."

"For Gawd's sake! What are you looking at me like that for? I'm not

188

strung out on the stuff. I only sniffed it once. You won't find marks on me. Look!" She thrust forward arms as smooth as alabaster.

"Where did you get it?" Alison tried not to sound as horrified as she felt.

"You must be joking, asking me that." Honey folded the packet in sulky silence and shoved it in her skirt pocket. "I was only trying to help. You looked like a wet dishcloth when I came in here."

Alison swallowed and said in a hushed voice, "You could be done for being in possession, Hon."

Honey yanked back the curtains and opened the window. She lit a cigarette and said from the side of her mouth, "Its *only* a fag!"

"I don't care what it is. I'm not your keeper."

"It's so easy for you, isn't it? You roll up here playing at being a waitress, then, at the end of summer, you'll toddle off back to poly where you'll be all nice and cosy. Well, it's not the same for the rest of us. We can't all escape to a comfy life when we've done our time here."

"I . . . "

"What do you think happens to me at the end of the summer, eh?"

"I thought you got another job?"

"Just like that!" Honey clicked her finger and thumb. "Ever thought what it's like looking for a job when you're a one-parent family? My mum don't have Brent in the winter, you know?"

Alison ran her fingers through the thick dark strands of her hair. "It must be very difficult."

"It is. And there's times when I think about what's coming and I want to escape from myself." She sniffed. There was a smudge of mascara on her cheek.

Alison felt sorry, and angry, and sad all at the same time. "Come on, Hon. Let's go for a walk. We both need it."

★ ★ ★

They stood on the beach and watched waves fizzing round their feet. Alison said hesitantly, "Suppose I could help you get a winter job? What would happen to Brent?"

Honey caught on quickly. "The hotel! You could ask Guy!"

"Remember, he's very unpredictable. Anyway, Neil manages the place."

"But you could try! You could try, Ali!" Honey pleaded.

"Yes . . . yes, I could . . . but not while you're messing about with that stuff. You are bound to be found out . . . "

"I swear! I swear I've only tried it once. Oh! . . . what the hell!" Honey tightened her lips and pulled the package from her pocket. She screwed it up and threw it into the sea. It bobbed about like a tiny crumpled face spewed up with the froth.

"Satisfied? And before you ask, I haven't got any more. I could get some — but I won't."

"In Summerland?"

"Anywhere. All you need is the bread. But I said, I won't touch it again. *Especially* if you can help me get this job."

Two joggers in shorts wheezed past them.

Suddenly Alison wanted to be free of this conversation. "Come on!" she shouted and began to run along the flat stone-coloured sand.

Soon they were both splashing and running about with the exuberance of little kids let out of school. At last, they stopped, breathless, laughing and soaked.

"Look!" Honey hissed.

Alison's pulse bounded even harder as she saw Guy riding a horse towards them along the firm sand near the shore.

"Ask him about the job!" Honey urged.

Alison bit her lip. Was it madness to choose this moment to ask him for a favour? Because she knew, now, she must make a decision that could devastate his father. She had to. Too many people were at risk.

She was going to present her findings about the cliffs to the Council.

She closed her eyes, half hoping Guy would have vanished when she opened them. She wished with all her being she had never heard of Summerland. That she had never allowed Guy Kington to take hold of her heart.

7

SITTING astride his magnificent chestnut mare, Guy smiled down at them.

Honey giggled. "Archie would have a fit if he saw us so wet and bedraggled."

"How is your father?" asked Alison.

"He appears OK but you can never tell with Dad. We've got a nurse with him."

He pressed his strong thighs against the horse's quivering flanks to steady her. His long muscled arms glowed under the short-sleeved tawny T-shirt. He looked like a great bronze statue, thought Alison.

Honey glanced towards Alison, then at Guy. "I'd . . . er, I'd better be getting back."

"How are things with you, Honey?" asked Guy.

"Me? Oh, fine, Mr Kington." She

added hastily, "I've learnt my lesson all right. I won't be getting into any more tangles." She gave a coy smile.

"Good for you," he said.

"I've got to go, but *you* stay, Alison. I expect you've got *lots* to talk about."

As Honey skipped across the beach Guy swung himself down, his expressive blue eyes fixed on Alison. She was suddenly conscious of the white T-shirt clinging wetly to her body.

She decided to broach the subject of a job for Honey, but he interrupted her.

"I'm glad we're alone, Alison. I want to apologize."

Her mouth hung open, mid-sentence.

He continued, "I think I was rude to you when you had supper with us. I'm sorry. I hadn't meant to be. It . . . it was a rather strange sort of evening.

"Was Neil . . . ?"

"Am I forgiven?" He put his arm lightly across her back as they walked along the shore, leading his horse with the other hand.

Guy glanced towards her. "Neil's got a point you know. He sees me turning up like the prodigal son, and he's afraid Dad might decide to leave the hotel to me. No chance. Neither do I want it. Neil's worked hard on the place. There was a time Dad took it for granted I would take over the business but I never felt it was my line, yet when I was young I only managed the odd protest. He never forgave me for leaving."

"Why did you?"

"The sort of publicity I was getting, was not going to do much for bookings. But you know that, of course."

"I heard you joined the Marines?"

"Eventually. Did all sorts of things first."

"And then you were wounded in the Falklands?"

"Only leg wounds."

"Then you started writing and became a rich man?"

He gave a short laugh. "You can be homesick in comfort when you've got money."

"Has your father read any of your books?"

"He's not one for reading. Even if I dedicated a book to him . . . and I never *do* dedicate books . . . you can be certain he still would not open it." He eyed his horse as it pawed at the sand and then looked at Alison. "Ever ridden?"

"Years ago."

"Come on, I'll lead you."

He helped her mount the horse and, gradually, Alison began to enjoy herself.

Guy started running, then suddenly, to her acute amazement, he swung himself up behind her, jolting the breath out of her, circling her damp body with his arms as his hands held the reins, his taut muscles pressed against her.

They were soon galloping over deserted stretches of beach. Her breasts swung against his hard biceps. Alison couldn't decide whether her heart was pounding madly from fear or from the sense of vulnerability she felt at that

197

moment as his body pressed against her back and buttocks and their hips moved in unison.

Almost against her will she felt an intense excitement growing inside her.

The farther they rode, the more it was patently obvious that no saddle fitted two people.

When he slowed down at last and slid to the ground, Alison's cheeks were on fire.

"That wasn't funny!" She was out of breath and her words were choked out.

"I thought you'd enjoy a burst of speed," he remarked wryly.

She was confused. Was that all it had been?

"I'll walk back," Alison mumbled.

"Oh, don't worry, you don't have to ride her again if you don't want to. I've got a car parked where I stable her." Guy patted the horse fondly when he left her at the stables on the outskirts of Summerland. "I shall miss her when I go away again."

"Does Neil ride?" Alison tried to sound matter-of-fact, but his remark was a jolting reminder that Guy wasn't there to stay.

"He prefers what he calls more 'aesthetic pursuits', like ice-skating, dancing. Here borrow this until you dry out."

He yanked a black sweater from the car. It buried her like a long floppy sack. She hoisted up the sleeves and was about to get in the car when he touched her arm.

"Can we walk for a little while?"

There was something about his earnest expression that made her agree. Alison was astounded when, as they were walking along the country lanes overlooking the sea, Guy brought up the subject of Debbie.

She murmured, "You didn't want her name mentioned."

"Believe it or not, I intended to get you on your own after supper to talk to you about her. But it didn't work out that way. I'd like to fill you in on what you may *not* have heard."

"Please . . . it doesn't matter."

"I've discovered it *does* matter to me what you think." His eyes met hers. He needed to talk. And he needed to talk to *her*.

Guy continued, "Debbie and I went out together — off and on. One day she rang in a hell of a state and asked if we could go somewhere private. We went over to the lighthouse. We knew we weren't supposed to go over there, but that didn't worry us. We'd been over plenty of times, away from Archie's prying eyes."

"Didn't he approve of you seeing one another?"

"He didn't approve of her seeing *any* male. Treated her like a precious ornament. No one was allowed to touch Debbie!"

"She behaved oddly that day. Oh, I was used to her moods, frivolous, petulant — but this was different. Eerily so. The minute we went into the lighthouse, she began to act out a

200

little seduction scene."

He gazed beyond a tangle of hawthorn bushes to the electric-blue sea.

"God knows why I didn't accept the invitation. She was wearing the scantiest underwear I'd ever seen. Perhaps I sensed the air of desperation about her. Or perhaps I liked to be the one who called the tune. I don't remember. But I do remember being puzzled by the strange expression in her eyes. She seemed to be on a different plane."

Alison could see it was painful for him to recall the incident. But he went on in a parched voice, "Then she told me she was pregnant. I said, 'Whose is it, Deb?' She started laughing. She said in a silly teasing voice, 'Well it could be yours if you want.' I demanded to know but she just floated around the room, waving her arms, saying, 'It's the stars', the moon's, a child of the heavens.'

"I wanted to shake her! I asked if that was why she'd wanted me to make love to her? To make damn sure I'd be in the line-up of paternity contenders?"

He brought his hand across his mouth as if wanting to wipe the words away forever.

Alison was silent as they walked along the dusty lane. To one side of them were long narrow gardens leading to a row of cottages, some of them empty. To the other side were shale and marl cliffs with a sheer drop to a golden beach with a grey quicksand collar where it touched slurry. Across the lane ahead of them was an old red and white barrier with its paint peeling and sunshine stuttering through its slats.

"I told her I was taking her back. She refused to budge." Guy's voice became a whisper. "I've asked myself a thousand times why I didn't stay and talk with her about her problems. But I said I'd wait for her at the boat . . . I was sure she'd follow me.

"I was outside when I heard the most chilling sound of my life. A sort of

202

high-pitched chanting. I looked up and saw her on the gallery. I raced up as fast as I'd ever run. I'd nearly reached her when she opened her arms, laughing, calling to me . . . calling . . . 'Watch me Guy. I can fly!' And . . . and, she jumped."

Alison put her hand on his arm. He choked "I felt as responsible as if I'd pushed her."

"But — wasn't she on drugs?"

"I should have realized. Stayed with her."

"We always torture ourselves about what we should have done *after* the event. I know I did after my mother died. We shouldn't. We can't change anything. We can only hurt ourselves."

He was silent after that, staring out to sea. Suddenly as if grimly determined to change the subject, he said, "That's enough about Debbie. Tell me about you. Tell me about your project."

Alison nodded towards the barrier. "I suppose that's what it's all about." She went to the barrier and climbed over it.

"Careful!" Guy warned.

She craned her graceful neck to gaze out beyond the jagged overhang where the road appeared to have been sliced across.

"Wow! The road drops to nothing!"

Guy followed her and stared down to the abyss. Around them were slavering biscuit and bronze-coloured cliffs.

"They're being eaten away," he murmured.

"Springs permeating the cliffs. Tidal surges. With the greenhouse effect there's a rise in sea level. I see there are coastal defences — revetments . . . "

"Did you know unexploded bombs from the last war have sometimes been found on these beaches?" Guy broke in. "I'd think twice about building a house here."

"But, Guy, don't you know the hotel could be in a similar situation? Given the right conditions, even though they may be freak ones."

She remembered how worried she'd been when she'd left the library after reading about events that could lead to a disaster on a coast such as this.

"All right, then let me judge for myself. Let me read your thesis," Guy said.

"I . . . "

"What's the matter? Not ready to have all those academic theories aired?"

Alison hesitated again. She realized she could no longer postpone what she had to tell him. It would hardly put him in a receptive mood to talk about Honey's job, she thought.

"As a matter of fact, I am. You see, I intend to show my thesis to the Council. I think they should know how dangerous — to my mind — the . . .

"Can I read it first?" Guy interrupted.

"Well . . . yes. Of course."

"I hope there aren't too many big words," he said with a wry smile.

She gave a light explosive laugh, as much from relief at his reaction as anything. He put his arms around her and turned towards the barrier. Now, get yourself back where it's safe. I think you must get a kick out of being in dangerous situations."

She'd crossed over to the other side, when she heard a crash. She spun round in alarm.

"Guy!" she screamed.

The road beyond the barrier had collapsed in an avalanche of mud and shingle, taking Guy with it.

"G-U-Y!" Her cry mingled with those of screeching seagulls sailing over the cliffs.

She heard his strangled voice. "Keep away from the edge!"

He was alive! She flew along the lane to an occupied cottage. The owner rang the coastguard. "The Mobile Rescue Unit's coming."

Alison raced down to the beach, leaping over slurry settled like paste at the foot of the cliffs.

Guy was spread-eagled part-way down. He hung on to what looked like a clump of weed. Alison bargained with God for his safety. Oh, let him hold on until rescue came! It didn't matter if he went back to Greece *tomorrow*. If she never saw him again. Only, let him be safe.

★ ★ ★

"How's Mr Guy?" said Cliff's nurse when Alison arrived at the hotel after driving the car back.

"Thank goodness they got to him before he fell any farther. But he has to stay in hospital, as I told you on the phone. He's done something to his arm — and he may have concussion."

"There's been hell let loose here. We've had reporters bombarding us with questions. Old Mr Kington didn't like that at all. Fancy us having a famous author in the place."

"How did they find out?"

"It seems someone at the hospital recognized Mr Guy from a photo on one of the books he was reading. The reporters were asking Mr Kington about some girl called Debbie."

"That's exactly what Guy wanted to

207

avoid. He said the gossip wouldn't do the hotel's reputation any good."

"Oh I don't know. A bit of gossip can do wonders for a place. I must say though, it didn't help the old man's temper. He wasn't too happy even *before* he knew about Mr Guy . . . " She stopped and gazed towards the staircase.

Alison was surprised to see Tracy on the stairs. The girl's expression was taut, cheeks stained. She hurried down, past the two women.

"Tracy . . . " began Alison.

"Buzz off!" Tracy ran past her to the door.

"They've been quarrelling again," remarked the nurse.

"I thought I heard your voice!" Clifford Kington appeared in the hallway gripping a piece of paper and leaning on his stick, his cheeks flaccid and grey.

"I came to tell you Guy is feeling a little better now," said Alison.

"We have been in touch with the

hospital ourselves, thank you," he replied curtly. There was a coldness in his tone that puzzled her.

"He didn't want you to worry about him. Fortunately he didn't fall down the steepest part of the cliffs, but it was very frightening."

"He'd know how to handle himself in any fall. He fought in the Falklands, you know?"

Did she detect a hidden pride in Guy? Cliff continued, "He's self-reliant, sure of himself. Not sure of women though. Doesn't trust 'em. And he has good cause!" He glared at her.

"I expect he'll find a woman he can trust one day. Settle down with her," Alison declared.

"Oh no. He'll never marry." He left unsaid the words, especially you. But Alison knew he was thinking them. What was wrong with him? He was suddenly so antagonistic towards her. He continued coldly, "So you were with Guy when he fell? And you the expert who knows all about cliffs!"

"No. Not an expert, Mr Kington . . . "

"But that doesn't stop you stirring things, does it?" He shook the sheet of paper under her nose.

She backed away, frowning. "What do you mean?"

"Don't pretend you don't know."

"I don't know!"

"*This* is only to advise me that a surveyor is being sent from the Council to poke his snotty nose around *my* premises! That's all! *Supposed* danger from erosion of cliffs etc. And you pretend you've had nothing to do with this?"

"I've told you . . . I don't know . . . " She stopped. Oh yes, perhaps she did know. Hadn't Simon said he was going to see Archie the last time he came to see her? He must have given Archie his findings about the cliffs. Archie had obviously wasted no time in contacting the Council, probably telling them the hotel was not safe.

"I can see by the guilty expression on your face that you knew. And you didn't have the decency to tell me you were going to the Council . . . and you came as a guest in my home!"

"Mr Kington," she said quietly, "I did not go to the Council, but I have to tell you I *did* intend doing so. I also intended telling you first."

"You knew I'd had my own survey done!" He waved the paper over his head while the nurse hovered anxiously nearby. "So do members of the Council. It's fairly obvious some jumped up little toad over there — who knows nothing at all about me! — is trying to carve out a niche for himself. Or herself. Yes, most likely some meddlesome woman who's new, with big ideas."

"With a hotel full of people, I wouldn't have thought you'd have objected to second opinions."

"Object? Me? Oh, I don't object at all. The thing I don't like is the underhand way it's been done." He leaned towards Alison with spittle in the corners of his mouth. The air between them shimmered with anger. He hissed, "There are folk round here who've yet to find out the sort of man they're dealing with."

In the silence that followed, Alison heard a small gasp from the nurse.

Neil stood at the top of the stairs, pale and limp. He gave an odd whimper, his naked body folded like a rumpled sheet.

"Drunk again, damn it!" rasped Cliff.

The nurse hurried up the stairs to Neil.

★ ★ ★

Alison left the hotel feeling miserable. Never in a million years would Cliff believe she would have told him first, before going to the Council.

The evening was sultry. Not a breath of wind. As Alison walked along the moon-pale path she thought, once again, that a light flickered from the lighthouse.

Stars, she told herself.

212

But she was not mistaken about the helicopter buzzing over the island.

When Alison returned to the chalet, Honey said eagerly, "Any hopes for a job?"

"It wasn't the right moment to ask, Hon. But I promise I will when Guy comes out of hospital."

"Hospital?"

Alison told her what had happened, finishing despondently, "If I hadn't been stupid and gone past the barrier in the first place, it wouldn't have happened."

"Come off it. Can you honestly see Guy Kington going anywhere he didn't want to go?"

"His father is none too pleased about reporters homing in on him . . . among other things," she added dolefully.

"It's all publicity."

"I don't think he wants publicity of any kind."

"Come to think of it, he doesn't advertise the hotel, but he's not short of money is he?"

213

"No," said Alison slowly. "He doesn't seem to be."

★ ★ ★

The next day after the midday meal, both of them dragged their aching feet back to the chalet, pulled off their clothes and sank on the beds.

"It's stifling!" gasped Honey.

"Good for next year's bookings."

"They'll flock here anyway with all the fantastic alterations Archie's got planned. Wouldn't mind a holiday here myself!"

There was a loud rap on the door. Honey grunted but didn't move, except to drag a sheet over herself and nod to Alison to open the door. Alison was astonished to see Guy with his arm in a sling. Her heart leaped. But he was unsmiling.

"You . . . you should be in hospital . . ."

"Waste of time. I'm perfectly fit now."

"Then what's the sling for?"

"God knows. I've only sprained the tendons."

Honey's voice trilled out, "For heaven's sake, get him in here before Archie sees him!"

"I'm not the least concerned whether Archie sees me or not. It's his daughter I'm looking for. Can you tell me where I can find her?"

"Why do you want her?" Honey poked her head round the door. She was wearing the sheet like a sarong. "She's trouble. Come in."

Guy's face looked like bleached leather. Alison felt concerned about him. He was obviously not fit to be running about.

"Tracy could be anywhere, Guy."

"The house? Archie's house?"

"You're bonkers. When Archie sees you he'll go mad." Honey twisted a tighter knot into the top of the sheet.

"Won't it wait?" said Alison, knowing full well he'd do exactly as he intended.

"It will not. I'm probably doing *him* a service."

215

"Is this to do with Neil being drunk?" asked Alison softly.

"He wasn't drunk."

Suddenly the door crashed open. Archie stood with military precision, glaring at Guy.

"What the bloody hell are you doing in my camp?"

"Looking for your daughter," replied Guy in a deep even voice.

Alison glowered at Archie. "It's usual to knock."

He shoved his forefinger towards her. "The less you say, the better for you. Bloody fine goings-on!" He glared at Honey who stood motionless, her mouth open. The sheet had slid further down to reveal ample cleavage.

Guy rounded on him. "Don't be stupid, man. For once in your life, listen to somebody else."

"Listen to who? You? Who killed my Debbie?" ranted Archie.

"He didn't kill her!" Alison faced Archie furiously.

"Oh yes? And what do you know

216

about it, eh? Got his word have you?
And you believed him?"

"Archie . . . " began Honey tremu-
lously, stepping towards him.

"Make yourself decent, you little . . . "
As Archie made to push her out of the
way, Guy grabbed him by the shoulder
with his free hand.

"Leave her alone. And listen!" His
grip on Archie tightened. The two
men glowered at one another. Guy
hissed, "I've reason to believe drugs
are being passed around — in this
camp, centre, whatever you like to call
it. Now, do you want your daughter,
Tracy, involved in it?"

Archie blanched. His voice became
a hoarse whisper. "You're a damned
liar, Kington."

"Someone close to me is involved.
I'm determined to find out where the
stuff is coming from."

"Ah-huh. So now the boot's on the
other foot, is it? So now it's *you* who's
searching for the answers, just like I did
all those years ago. Well, I'll tell you

now, you can forget trying to implicate anyone in *my* place. I run a good clean holiday centre — and my little girl knows exactly what would happen to her if she ever so much as touched that poison."

"I'm not saying she takes it, man! But she might know something about it. Surely, if there's anything going on here you would want the matter cleared up?"

"I tell you, there's *nothing* like that here!" Archie shouted.

"There is Archie," said a tiny voice. They all looked at Honey. Archie screwed up his face. "What the hell are you saying?"

"There is stuff here, if you want it."

Guy let go of Archie and turned towards Honey. He said quietly, "How does it get into the place, Honey?"

"Don't know." She pouted.

"But you've damn well used it, haven't you?" barked Archie.

"I haven't! I haven't! Tell him, Alison."

Alison found herself muttering something incomprehensible.

"Well, has she?" demanded Archie.

"Tell them how you got it, Hon," Alison said.

Honey ran her small pink tongue over her lips to wet them. "I was only *offered* it."

"Who?" urged Guy softly.

Honey became suddenly sullen. "A bloke I know."

"*Who*?" This time it was Archie probing.

"A bloke I know."

"And I bet you know quite a few!" said Archie derisively. He looked at Guy. "You can't believe what *she* says."

Alison looked at the woe-begone expression on Honey's face; the ridiculous sad way she clung to the sheet; the helplessness. She cried, "Don't talk to her like that! You treat women as if we're some lower species!"

"I treated you good! I give you time

off to do all that college work."

"Only because there was something in it for you. Now you've got what you want, I shall be surprised if you give me another job. You couldn't wait to give Simon's findings to the Council, could you?"

"I don't know what the devil you're talking about — but you're right about the job." He pointed a stubby finger at Honey. "And I ain't having her back either!"

"I don't need it!" countered Honey. "I expect Guy can get me a job at the hotel."

"I most certainly will," said Guy after the briefest pause.

His words seemed to put new hope into Honey as she faced Archie defiantly. "I hope for your sake, the police never find out . . . "

"Watch what you're saying! I'll have you up for slander," spat Archie.

"All right then, if you don't believe me, try keeping an eye on the laundry van that comes here on

Saturday morning — and that shed where Maurice keeps his boat . . . " She stopped, realizing she'd said too much. Archie stared at her, then turned abruptly and rushed from the chalet.

"Oh hell; that's done it!" Honey dropped heavily on the bed.

"Where is this boat-shed?" asked Guy.

"You aren't going there now?"

"No one is going to be fool enough to be messing about in there while the beach is crowded," said Guy.

"Even if you did find anything, Archie would never believe you."

When Guy left them he was grim and preoccupied.

Honey's gaze followed him. "He's all man, that one. All man! But I wish I hadn't told Archie about the drugs."

"You were very brave."

"Sod being brave. That's what I say."

That night when Alison was sure Honey was asleep she crept out of bed and put on a butter-coloured dress.

She hoped she would blend in with the colours of the sand dunes.

Her sandals sank in the sand. She could hear the soft whoosh of waves on the beach. She positioned herself where she could see the hut where Maurice's boat was kept.

Suddenly there was a sound behind her. She froze.

"What the devil are you doing here at this time of the night?" hissed Guy.

Her body relaxed. She whispered, "It was me who persuaded Honey to tell what she knew. Now I'm going to find out for myself and corroborate her story." She hesitated before adding, "And I guessed you might come out here when it was dark. There has to be a witness if you want to convince Archie."

"And you think he'll take notice of you?" Guy allowed himself a wry smile.

"I'm better than no witness at all, aren't I?"

He put his free arm gently round her. Even a touch so soft made her nerve-endings tingle. He said, "There's no one in the hut at the moment and I don't even know if there will be."

"I'm prepared to wait."

"Come into this hollow where we won't be seen."

They were surrounded by marram grass. Their whispered voices seemed to echo in the still night.

"Thanks for going to hospital with me," Guy said gently.

"If it hadn't been for me, you wouldn't have gone past that silly barrier in the first place."

"Of course not." His voice was deeply solemn but she knew he was teasing her.

She blushed. "D-does your arm hurt a lot?"

"Look." He took the sling off, flexed his arm gently and moved it in a slow circle. His bare muscles were long and sinewy. He lifted his hand and stroked her cheek. She told herself it was the oppressive heat that made her suddenly very hot. There was thumping inside her. His thumb traced the outline of her lips.

"You have very inviting lips," he murmured.

"It . . . it d-doesn't look as if anyone is coming to the boat-shed after . . . "

The sentence was never finished. He drew her tightly against him. His chest was like iron. Her bones became liquid fire.

His mouth was soft and sensuous; his tongue probed her. She felt vulnerable, like the cliffs with their soft slurry undermining their stability. Her body rocked against him as they kissed. She tried to be silent but she made odd strangled noises.

He held her even tighter. She knew now there was no way she wanted to remember what anyone had said about him. There was one moment in her life. This was that moment.

He stroked her; explored her. The

soft sand cradled them. She touched his injured arm and whispered, "Be careful. You'll hurt it."

"Nothing is going to hurt, darling. I promise," he murmured hoarsely.

8

IT was in the early hours when they heard sounds on the beach. A faint glow came from the boat-shed as three figures disappeared in there.

"I'm going to see what's happening," Guy whispered.

"Me too."

"No. You stay here." Guy crept across the dunes.

She jumped as a voice behind her growled, "And what do you think you're doing, eh?"

"Archie!"

"Waiting for Kington, I'll be bound!" His sharp eyes followed her gaze towards the boat-shed. "So that's it, is it? He's come to do the same as me. Find out if Honey was talking out of the back of her head."

There was a sudden commotion as

Guy opened the door. Two figures raced out of the hut. Guy ran after the one who flew like the wind in the direction of the hotel.

Archie charged after the other who headed for the dunes . . . a man who, Alison thought, resembled the laundry van driver who called at Summerland.

She ran to the hut and stared inside. A candle flickered in a tin. There was a strange smell like there had been in the lighthouse.

From a shadowy corner behind the boat, a bedraggled figure rose slowly to his feet. His eyes were heavy.

"Hi, Alison," he muttered before slithering to the ground again. Alison gaped.

Archie panted up behind her. "I'll never catch him. He's disappeared in the dunes . . . " He screwed up his eyes and walked round the boat.

"Bloody-hell. Jack!"

"Let's get out of here," he growled to Alison.

Outside there was no sign of Guy

or anyone else and Archie insisted on escorting Alison back to her chalet.

She couldn't sleep. Thoughts jumped in her head like sand-fleas. How could Jack and the others have risked so much? But overriding everything were her thoughts of Guy. He had roused her to fever pitch with his expert lovemaking. And afterwards, when she had thought it was all over . . . The exquisite thrill of how it had been would stay with her always.

★ ★ ★

The next day, gossip was rife.

Honey chatted excitedly. "You won't believe it, Ali. Jack has been sacked! After all these years. Why would Archie do that? There won't be any of us left, soon. And that's not all. Janet heard Archie and Rita having a row. Fancy Rita arguing! Archie's found out his precious daughter has been dating Neil Kington. He's packed Tracy off to her auntie's . . . "

Alison took her project file to the hotel.

"Another baking day," the receptionist said to Alison. "The forecast is for a break in the weather, but I can't see it myself."

Guy was in his father's study. He kissed her gently. She looked into his sad, troubled face. "What's wrong, Guy?"

"Dad's taken himself to London."

"Is he fit enough?"

"No way. He left a note. He doesn't want any of us following him . . . I expect you've guessed it was Neil I chased from the boat-shed? We had a row. Dad heard." He ran his fingers through his thick wiry hair. "I'd suspected for some time Neil might be on drugs. When I got home from hospital and heard he'd collapsed I had to find out the truth once and for all. I love my brother. The next time he collapses might be the last.

"Before Dad walked in on us, Neil admitted he got the stuff from a guy

229

who called at your place. Refused to say, who. But he *has* told me Tracy isn't into that scene."

"Do you think he's trying to shield her?"

"I doubt he's interested enough in women to do that." He sighed. "It's all falling into place: his swings of mood, his arguments . . . "

"And I accused you of not standing up to him. Why don't I learn to mind my own damn business? You can't argue with someone who's high."

"I shouldn't have tried last night, then Dad wouldn't have heard us. But then I would never have known . . . " He stopped, his expression grim. "None of us knows the first thing about one another when it boils down to it. Even our own families." His eyes were dead. "Be glad you aren't involved in any way with mine."

"B-but I am."

"Alison, you do know I shall be leaving for Greece soon?"

"Oh? You must like it very much."

Her mouth was dry.

"Life is more relaxed out there. The press don't bother me. The old man didn't like it at all when they swarmed in on him."

"I expect he didn't want the story of you and Debbie dredged up again."

"Or anything else that would bring publicity to the hotel," he said bitterly.

A window pane rattled. Outside a rose bush dragged its nails along the glass as a breeze blew up.

Alison put her project file on the desk.

"I — I only came to give you this."

When Guy answered the telephone and she signalled she was leaving, he didn't try to stop her.

★ ★ ★

That evening she wandered despondently along the cliff-walk. The day had been extremely humid but now a wind thrashed hedges; grass rippled in the moonlight. It was daylight bright. She watched the foaming waves hitting at sea-defences, and frowned. The tide was unusually high.

"A-L-I-S-O-N!" came a cry.

Alison stared in the direction of the hotel then started to run to the steps leading to the beach. Tracy was halfway down them, trying to support Neil's dead weight.

"Can you help me? I reckon he's drunk or something!" cried Tracy.

Between them they half dragged Neil's limp body. At the top of the steps he started to giggle.

"It's not bloody funny!" spat Tracy.

"I'm a' right." He meandered dangerously close to the cliff edge.

Alison was thankful when she saw Guy. He was climbing into the Range-Rover but rushed across when he spotted them. He clamped his sound arm around his brother, almost lifting him bodily.

"OK . . . you're OK. Lean on me," Guy said gently.

Once indoors, Neil seemed to brighten

232

up but Cliff's nurse and Guy took him upstairs. Alison heard the nurse say, "Don't worry, I'll stay with him while you're gone."

Tracy muttered to Alison, "I'm staying too. I want to be here when he sobers up. There's no way I'm going back to my auntie's. Dad's punishing me for what happened to Debbie."

Alison was about to leave when she saw Guy hurrying down the stairs.

"Surely you aren't driving?"

"I have to."

"But your arm . . ."

"I'll manage. I've had a call from London. Dad's in hospital. He's had a heart attack. I have to go there."

★ ★ ★

Alison managed to persuade Guy to let *her* drive the Range-Rover.

She was surprised he'd brought along her thesis; surprised that he seemed to have read most of it already.

After an acid-yellow streak zigzagged

the sky, a clap of thunder made her grip the steering wheel tightly. Tree-tops on either side of them were bending in the rising gale. Then rain started hammering on the roof.

"The weather's broken now all right." She tried not to sound nervous.

He went on reading and murmured, "I noticed the barometer falling."

She was almost driving blind as the windscreen wipers fought the deluge so she pulled into the next lay-by. Guy was staring at her file with a glazed expression.

"This makes a lot of sense, Alison," he said slowly. He sounded concerned. She told herself he'd got enough to worry about already and said, "Well, fortunately your father had his own survey done of the hotel."

"Oh, yes. He had a survey done."

She was puzzled by his cynical tone. He took a deep breath. "I didn't tell you quite how distraught my father was last night when he found out Neil was a junkie. Afterwards, when we were alone

234

he broke down completely. It was as if he couldn't stop talking. A pity he left it so late before . . . " He bit his lip.

He continued acidly, "It appears my father was in a position to bribe — blackmail — call it what you like, some eminent people in this community. And now — when I read this . . . " He nodded towards the file.

"I don't understand."

"You are absolutely right. The hotel *COULD* be in danger. Particularly in conditions like tonight's."

"But the survey . . . "

"Exactly. How do we know the guy who did it wasn't one of those in the palm of Dad's hand? That he gave just the report that was wanted? A bent report!"

"It isn't possible!"

"Believe me, anything is possible. I've discovered that much in the last twenty-four hours." He gazed out at the belting rain and the lightning, then back at her file. "I've left a hotel full of guests . . . a hotel that may not be as safe as I thought.

"We're going back, Alison."

She tried not to speed on the wet roads, but her mind was on the high tide she'd seen that night, the change of wind direction — and other factors that, combined, just might be the agents of destruction.

They saw flashing lights ahead of them. When they slowed down they heard the hum of saws. A sopping wet policeman walked to the side of the Range Rover. "Sorry, miss, I'm afraid you'll have to divert. There's a tree across the road."

Guy directed her along a muddy track with more dangerously leaning trees. She only relaxed when she was back driving on the coast road.

They were nearly back at Summerland when she gave a sharp intake of breath.

"Stop!" shouted Guy. But she'd already hit the brakes. Guy peered at the road ahead. "Who the hell was the imbecile standing in the middle of the road? Where's he gone?"

"Did you see what he was wearing?" she gasped.

"I don't give a damn . . . "

"He was dressed like a Roman soldier!"

"If some lunatic who's been to a fancy-dress party wants to thumb lifts . . . "

"But you must have heard the story? The Roman soldier who appears when there's going to be a disaster?"

"Complete rubbish."

"Then where is he now?"

Guy zipped up his jacket and climbed out with his head down against the wind and rain. He walked a short way along the road and then returned, his expression grim.

"I don't know who that guy was — but he just saved our lives. Half the road is missing. It's collapsed with the cliff."

Alison's hands were trembling as she turned on the hazard lights. "Where's the nearest phone?"

"The hotel. It isn't far now. We can get by on foot."

They began to run the rest of the way.

"Guy! Look! The sea defences have been breached!"

They only slowed down when they saw the hotel standing strong and safe.

"Thank God!" he exclaimed. They stood for a moment, out of breath, and then ran again until they reached the wasteland beside the hotel. Guy put his arm round her. "I'll be taking no more chances after this. Tomorrow I'll clear the place and get my own survey done." He blew into his cheeks. "Never thought I'd be glad to see it!"

The explosion knocked them both off their feet.

The path at the rear of the hotel between the garden and the cliffs had collapsed. There was a sheer drop to the boiling sea. But Alison's horrified gaze was rivetted on the garden itself. There was a gaping hole where the earth had split open.

She gasped as the conservatory began to crumble into it. She could hear glass splintering through the wailing wind. Potted plants and basket-chairs plummeted to nowhere.

Guy had rushed inside the hotel, ripping off his arm-sling and ordering her not to follow him. But now she flew round to the front of the building and up the steps.

Staff were shepherding guests outside to the veranda. Some had grabbed waterproofs to wear over their night-clothes. Did they know the back of the building was disintegrating?

Alison was helping more guests to leave the hotel when she saw a pale panic-stricken Kedrun trying to wrap a bandage around a guest's finger. Kedrun gave a frantic whisper. "Guy asked me to see to this man. He's cut his finger. Guy KNOWS I can't stand the sight of blood!"

"Would you like me . . . ?"

"Oh, please, Alison. I'm not feeling

239

so good myself. I'll go and sit in the car for a bit. If you want me . . . ?"

Alison nodded and was tending to the man when someone shouted, "Where's my little boy?"

She heard Tracy answer, "I've got him. He's OK." Then Tracy turned to Neil and snapped at him, "For God's sake, move a bit faster, you! You must have sobered up by now!"

There were screams as a chandelier in the dining-room smashed to the floor. The receptionist said to Alison, "I can't get Mrs Bennet to come downstairs."

Alison finished tying the bandage and went to Mrs Bennet's room.

"I've lost my reading glasses. I must find them. Will you see if they're under the bed, dear?" she said. Alison dived under the bed. A moment later the old lady cried, "Here they are! Under my pillow. Aren't I silly?"

As Alison escorted her down the stairs, Mrs Bennet babbled "My word, this is going to be something to talk about when I go home. I say! Look at that! There used to be a fireplace there. I hope someone has telephoned the fire brigade about all this . . . "

Alison did not tell her the lines were down.

Outside, she heard Archie's loud voice before she saw him.

"Ladies and gentlemen! Summerland holiday centre is open to all of you. Hot baths, drinks for everyone, dry clothes . . ."

"Alison!"

Alison turned to see Rita, wet and dishevelled, rain running down her anxious face. "Someone said Tracy's here. If Archie finds out she . . . "

The hotel seemed to lurch. There was a deafening crash. Then a loud scream from upstairs. Alison rushed back up there. Guy was standing in an open doorway. Tracy was crouched on the opposite side of the room. Except for a narrow joist the floor between them had disappeared.

"Look at me, Tracy. DON'T look

down. Stand up." Guy was talking in a deep soothing voice.

"I can't," Tracy was trembling with fear.

"Yes you can."

"I bloody well can't!"

"Stand up!"

Tracy slowly stood up, her eyes wide and staring. She pressed her hands flat against the cracked wall behind her.

Alison saw how taut Guy's shoulder-blades were under his wet shirt. He spoke softly again. "I know you've got plenty of courage, Tracy. I've seen how you behaved tonight, helping the guests. The time has come to help yourself now. OK?"

Tracy stifled a sob and nodded.

"I want you to edge yourself along a couple of steps and you'll be at the end of the joist."

"What?"

"Move this way a bit."

"No! No! I'm scared of heights!"

"Don't look down."

"I'm going to die!" she shrieked.

Guy murmured to Alison, "Stand here. I'm going across. Hold your arm out and take a firm hold of her the minute she's close enough. Hang on to the door handle to steady yourself."

He balanced himself on the joist and after a moment, began to walk slowly across to Tracy. Alison held her breath as she watched him. Somewhere in the distance she could hear sirens. Then Archie's voice whispered in her ear, "I'll steady her this end. You hold on to me."

His leathery face had a bleached look about it and was a mass of lines.

It seemed like a lifetime to her before Guy had coaxed Tracy to step on to the joist. He held her waist from behind.

"I can't!" she yelled.

"Course you can, gel," croaked Archie. He had his arms stretched towards her while Alison gripped his waist.

"Walk to your dad, Tracy. It's only a few steps. I've got you." Alison heard an unusual tremor in Guy's voice. She tried to swallow but her mouth was too dry.

At last, Tracy began the long slow walk across the joist. But there was a moment when Guy had to release his hold on her — and Archie could not reach her. Tracy froze.

"Come on, gel, Neil's waiting for you." Archie's voice was no more than a whisper. Tracy wobbled. She stepped forward and caught hold of her father's hands. Archie dragged her backwards with him through the doorway. His body fell against Alison's. He put his arms around Tracy and held her tightly, then turned to Alison.

"Take her outside, will you?"

She saw the tears glistening on his cheeks.

When Alison looked back, he was leaning towards Guy with his arms outstretched.

She thanked God that the hotel had been cleared, when there was the sound of rending timber and crashing brickwork. She watched, mesmerized, as the chimney opened and collapsed with the roof. Slowly the back half of the hotel crumbled into the sea.

It was after that, that the rain stopped.

★ ★ ★

Whatever else anyone was feeling, Archie was on a high. He continued to rush around informing everyone, including the firemen who'd got the last of the guests out, that his facilities were at everyone's disposal.

Guy was hurrying between guests and organizing where they would like to stay for the rest of the night. There were many offers from other hotel owners and residents of Summerland. Guy would try to arrange transport for any guests who wanted to return home immediately.

Although he was being calm and reassuring, there was an unhappy, tormented expression in his eyes. Alison had once seen him wince when someone accidently knocked his arm. But this expression had nothing to do with physical pain.

"Miss Lacie? Could I have a word, please?"

She turned to see a fresh-faced reporter. He said, "I believe it was you who predicted this hotel was unsafe?"

"I didn't exactly go around telling everyone . . ."

"But you did think it unsafe?"

"This whole coastline is very vulnerable. The rate of erosion is increasing . . ."

"In your opinion?"

"Of course in my opinion." She was in no mood to start discussing all this.

"But you aren't qualified?"

"I happen to be studying . . ."

"Don't you think you might have caused a lot of unnecessary panic, spreading rumours about the hotel's safety? I mean — it did withstand the full force of the worst storm we've had in years."

Alison was flabbergasted by his remark. But then he continued, "After all, it did take a bomb to bring it down."

"What?" She stared.

"From the last war. Been hidden all these years. Amazing."

"Bomb?" she whispered.

"So have you any comment? It's only natural for our readers to wonder if anxiety about supposed cliff erosion here might have contributed to Mr Cliff Kington's heart attack — and his death tonight in London."

★ ★ ★

Alison was in the chalet packing when Archie knocked on the door.

"Terrible business last night. Terrible," he said.

She wondered how genuine Archie was. He *looked* genuine.

"Who'd have believed a bomb could do all that damage?"

She folded a jumper. "I don't believe

247

it was just the bomb. I still think it was a combination of factors . . . oh, never mind." She added ironically, "Well — I got myself in the papers after all. It was my ambition once, you know. Huh!"

"Now look, don't you go taking any notice of all that stuff they wrote about you."

"I really believe there would have been a disaster here sooner or later, bomb or no bomb. But I'll never be taken seriously until I've got myself qualified. And I see now what a heck of a lot of work I've got to do."

"Well. Them bits of paper make all the difference and it's no use pretending they don't."

She was feeling far from cheerful but couldn't help grinning. "Even for a woman, Archie?"

"What I came to say, Alison . . . well, I was a bit hasty when I said I wouldn't have you back, gel. At the time I was knocked sideways, hearing about drugs and pushers and everything, here in Summerland. I couldn't take that on board. I couldn't."

He took a bag of caramels out of his pocket and offered them to her. She shook her head. He looked into the bag, then screwed it up without taking a sweet out. "You know you can stay if you want to? And there's something else. I changed my mind about Guy Kington. He saved my Trace."

"And do you think, now, he's the sort of man who would have harmed Debbie?"

"He didn't." He shuffled awkwardly.

"What?"

"Seems Jack has been keeping a lot to himself. He said he was on the island the day Debbie died. He saw her fall. He said . . . he said, she opened her arms and launched herself. Nobody pushed her."

"Why has he kept that to himself all these years?" she gasped.

"He thought I wanted to protect my Debbie's reputation. That I didn't want folks knowing she committed suicide. So when I sounded off about the

249

Kingtons, he went along with me. Wanted to keep his job, did Jack. After I sacked him though, he didn't care what he said. He was always a crawler . . . he . . . he should have spoken up." His shoulders were bowed.

"I'm sorry, Archie."

"Best I know isn't it? Though I'm never going to know everything. Me and Rita have chucked all her stuff out of the attic at last. Found a diary. That was a shock. Seems it was some local lad got our Debbie pregnant. She says nothing in it about drugs so I don't suppose I'll ever know where she got the stuff. *I* reckon it was LSD. God knows where it came from. That bastard, Jack swears there were no drugs in the camp in those days."

Archie's eyes sparked. "I'm beginning to wonder if I know owt at all! I'll tell you one thing. I'll make good and sure my new centre is clean and decent for families! I'll vet every bloody member of my staff . . . !"

Alison felt curiously pleased to see the old Archie coming back to life. As he was leaving, he said, "Don't forget to let me have your thesis to read."

"Archie, who did go to the Council about the cliffs?"

"Nobody. It said in the papers — they were already planning to inspect all buildings near the beach. Huh. Funny when you think about it — you and me weren't going to blind 'em with science after all, were we? Still, it won't hurt for me to keep pushing for better sea and coastal defences. So let me see what you wrote. After all, you did it in my time!"

★ ★ ★

When Alison went to find Guy, she saw him wandering ghost-like in the grounds of his ruptured home.

"I'm so sorry about your father," she said softly.

"We wouldn't have got there in time. Must have been fate made us turn back." His face was creased with sadness, but as he turned her towards him she saw the spark of anger in his eyes. "I hope you realize that what was reported in the paper, was in no way the truth. Dad's death was not brought on by so called 'rumours' about the safety of the hotel."

"What I said to him about the cliffs could have contributed . . . "

"Listen, Alison. I'm going to tell you what really aggravated his illness." He took a long deep breath. "I found out before he left for London what was on his mind. He's been dealing in drugs — not touching them himself of course — and this hotel was the perfect spot where negotiations could take place. It had to stay that way. No publicity of any sort."

Alison stared. "D-did Neil know?"

Guy shook his head. "Nor me. I'd seen the odd stranger coming to the hotel, but I never dreamed . . . " He continued bitterly, "Why? In God's name, why? And who were his clients?

Old people? Youngsters?" Then, to himself, "Surveyors?"

Alison gazed miserably at the stained sky. She could hardly believe what he'd told her. The only comfort she could give was to listen while he spilled out the horror fermenting in him. He continued, "He went berserk when he discovered his own son was an addict. He spilled out all his sordid secrets.

"It seems the stuff was dropped on the island by helicopter. The laundry-van driver made pick-ups from there. He was in the lighthouse on the day you visited it. He didn't want to arouse any sort of suspicion by being there on his own so he got the hell out of it. Released your boat to delay you while he got out of sight. He's been running things while Dad has been ill; started dealing in the hard drugs — collected his own clients, Neil among them."

"What was Neil on?"

He won't say. It could have been just about anything. Dad swore he never dealt in hard drugs — but who's to believe anyone any more? All I know is that I want to see my brother happy and well again."

"Can anything be done for him?"

"I don't know. I've been told intensive counselling could help. But Neil himself has to decide to go to the rehabilitation centre. He might — when he reaches rock-bottom. If it's not too late, then.

"God! I'll never forgive the old man!"

They walked in silence to the beach.

After a while she said, "Why did Cliff rush off to London?"

"To meet Mr — or Mrs — Big. Close all deals, he said. There was too much publicity. The local press found out about me and my writing; Archie had got wind of what was going on on his patch. I expect Dad got cold feet."

"Or was it because he was suffering terrible remorse?"

"Bit late for that! Sorry, I shouldn't bark at you. I've been in two minds

254

about telling you all this, but I won't have you thinking for one minute that anything you said contributed to his heart attack. It was Neil he was distraught about."

"I still wish I hadn't sounded off about the cliffs, especially when it's said a bomb did all the damage here. It seems I've a great deal more to learn."

He turned quickly towards her.

"Listen. It's people like you who stir things up, who get the authorities moving. Didn't you read in the paper that intensive investigations are now going on all along this coast? How do you know it isn't because they heard about you and your project?"

She looked at him thoughtfully and then said hotly, "I still reckon it was all due to a combination of factors and not just the bomb. Look at the coast road!"

For a moment a brief smile hovered on his lips at her renewed belief in her own convictions. Then he turned to study the racing sea. "I suppose I should take a measure of comfort knowing Dad didn't get involved with drugs until after Debbie died.

"God knows why I believed him when he assured me of that — but I did." He sighed. "Some family, eh? I ask myself if things would have been different if I'd stayed here and taken my share of running the place."

"You know Neil liked to be top dog here."

"I've never seen Dad cry before," said Guy dully.

The breeze whipped at Alison's cheeks. She rubbed her hands up and down her bare arms. Guy glanced at her and peeled off his sage-green sweater. "Here — put this on." Its soft silky warmth enveloped her like an embrace.

He continued, "I thought it was odd. I found press cuttings about me in Dad's room. And the books I've written. I didn't think he ever read my books."

"I always had the feeling he wasn't able to show you how he really felt about you, Guy. Perhaps he didn't know himself. But I'm sure he was proud of you."

"The feeling isn't mutual." The voice didn't sound like Guy's.

His dark hair blew across his forehead. She saw him wipe the spray from the waves out of his eyes.

She knew he was going through his own private torment.

Suddenly he turned, seized hold of her hand and pulled her with him as they began to run back towards the hotel.

"I can't . . . I can't keep up with you!" she panted. "Guy . . . !" She wanted to laugh and cry and throw her arms around him all at the same time. He turned her to face him, gently rubbing his thumbs across her shoulders. She could feel the warmth of his breath. Her heart began to thud — but not from running.

"Look — I don't pretend to know

anything about rocks and things, but I do know a damned good piece of writing when I see it. And that's what your thesis is. Not biased in any way. An excellent report. I see a great future ahead of you Alison. It — it may not be the future you imagined for yourself . . . "

"Go on," she whispered hoarsely.

"The reporters *will* get it right. One day you'll get the press you deserve."

"Even in Greece?" She forced a laugh.

"Oh yes." His voice lowered. "And when I see your name, I shall tell everyone . . . I used to know her."

He pulled her to him and kissed her long and fiercely. She was not sure if the salty taste was from his lips or her own tears.

★ ★ ★

When Alison returned to polytechnic she tried to avoid the press but it was impossible. However, her thesis was highly praised by her tutor. At the same time a book was published on erosion written by an eminent professor and Alison was delighted that many of her findings were compatible with his.

After that she worked as she had never worked in her life. It helped to numb the awful ache inside her. This time there was no Simon to help. This time she learned to cope alone.

During the year, Honey wrote to her. Archie's new Summerland Holiday World was to be open all the year.

Before he'd left for Greece, Guy had persuaded Archie to have Honey back permanently.

'And Ali,' Honey wrote, 'I won't let him down. I'm a together person now. Not as though Archie hasn't got his little red eyes on me! But I got someone else to think about as well. Guess what. I got Brent with me! He's in the crèche when I'm working. Archie let him come. So I'd be a fool to mess things up, wouldn't I? This place is whiter than white what with

Jack buzzed off somewhere and the van-driver in prison. He won't beat up any more women like he did me for a long time.'

With each letter that arrived, Alison longed for news of Guy.

'Rita is groovy to work for, Ali,' she read. 'She gives me more time off than I had before. She runs her own little gift shop now. Had to battle with Archie, word has it. Ha ha! Good for her is what I say.

'Tracy's still at college. Found another boyfriend! Neil's been in some clinic. He's out now. Him and a friend are going to run a pub in the north. He got the dog back from Kedrun . . .'

Alison wondered why Guy never wrote to her. Had Honey been right all along? Had she merely been a chapter in his life?

She tried to forget about him but restless nights and endless dreams ravaged her good intentions.

★ ★ ★

Alison qualified with an honours degree. Simon turned up to congratulate her. He agreed with everyone else that she had a brilliant future ahead of her. In fact, he said, theirs could be a brilliant partnership. He told her he had split up with Renate.

Alison was in a bookshop when she saw a display of books by an author who had won a major prize.

CONTRACT IN MADRID by GUY KINGTON.

Her heart stopped. Guy! He'd written a book about drug smuggling. And he'd used his own name. But there was something else unusual. He had done what he said he never did. He had dedicated a book. She read: 'For my beloved Alison'.

Tears sprang to Alison's eyes. To hell with pride! She flew to the nearest phone. Archie was bound to know Guy's address.

★ ★ ★

It was sweltering in Athens. As she stepped off the plane the heat made Alison catch her breath. And so many people! Announcements in a language she didn't understand.

As she moved slowly through passport control her pulse raced. Then she couldn't find a trolley.

At last she saw the barrier where people waited for friends and relatives.

"Alison!"

Guy had vaulted over the barriers. He crushed her hard against him until she couldn't breathe. His mouth was over hers. He looked at her and cupped her face in his hands.

"I'll never let you go again!" He kissed her again and her bones liquidified.

A policeman standing talking to the girl from the sweet shop called out to Guy. Guy laughed and answered in Greek.

"What did he say?" asked Alison, her heart bursting with joy to be with him.

"I'll tell you when we're on honeymoon."

"You take a lot for granted!" she declared — but her smile was bewitching.

That night she gazed at the stars through the open window of his villa surrounded by orange groves. He'd said she could choose where they were to live. That all that mattered was being together. She ran her fingers over his brown skin.

For the first time in her life she knew exactly where she belonged.

THE END

WITH SOMEBODY ELSE
Theresa Charles

Rosamond sets off for Cornwall with Hugo to meet his family, blissfully unaware of the shocks in store for her.

A SUMMER FOR STRANGERS
Claire Hamilton

Because she had lost her job, her flat and she had no money, Tabitha agreed to pose as Adam's future wife although she believed the scheme to be deceitful and cruel.

VILLA OF SINGING WATER
Angela Petron

The disquieting incidents that occurred at the Vatican and the Colosseum did not trouble Jan at first, but then they became increasingly unpleasant and alarming.

DOCTOR NAPIER'S NURSE
Pauline Ash

When cousins Midge and Derry are entered as probationer nurses on the same day but at different hospitals they agree to exchange identities.

A GIRL LIKE JULIE
Louise Ellis

Caroline absolutely adored Hugh Barrington, but then Julie Crane came into their lives. Julie was the kind of girl who attracts men without even trying.

COUNTRY DOCTOR
Paula Lindsay

When Evan Richmond bought a practice in a remote country village he did not realise that a casual encounter would lead to the loss of his heart.